Jay Gummerman was born, raised and educated in California. He now lives in San Clemente. *We Find Ourselves in Moontown* is his first collection of stories.

Author photograph by Chris Gautner.

We Find Ourselves
in Moontown

Jay Gummerman

BLACK SWAN

WE FIND OURSELVES IN MOONTOWN

A BLACK SWAN BOOK 0 552 99388 3

Originally published in Great Britain
by Jonathan Cape Ltd.

PRINTING HISTORY

Jonathan Cape edition published 1989
Black Swan edition published 1990

This book is set in 12/14 pt Mallard
by Colset Private Limited, Singapore.

Black Swan Books are published by
Transworld Publishers Ltd., 61–63
Uxbridge Road, Ealing, London W5 5SA, in
Australia by Transworld Publishers
(Australia) Pty. Ltd., 15–23 Helles Avenue,
Moorebank, NSW 2170, and in New
Zealand by Transworld Publishers (N.Z.)
Ltd., Cnr. Moselle and Waipareira
Avenues, Henderson, Auckland.

Printed and bound in Great Britain by
Cox & Wyman Ltd, Reading

For Kelly

See here how ev'rything lead up to this day,
and it's just like any other day that's ever been.

Robert Hunter, *Black Peter*

Contents

We Find Ourselves in Moontown

FLAG DAY

Josephine as the Beehive State wants to know if it's possible to stub your nose. She's looking far away, maybe even Utah, and rubbing her bruised nose with a Honey Bear.

'Nothing's possible,' I tell her. I realize that's probably the wrong thing to say to a little girl, especially since I'm her teacher and her mother is eight months pregnant and five months my girl friend. But, hell, it's Flag Day, June 14th, the last day of school before summer, and I'm throwing a farewell costume party for my fifth-grade class at my house. Everybody is a star, a state in the United States of America. The teacher doesn't have to dress up. The teacher gets to be the deejay and drink beers and tell the truth about George Washington and generally carry on in a fashion not appropriate for a regular schoolday. We have Sly and the Family Stone and Steve and Eydie and Pablo Cruise. Lionel told me his mother wouldn't let him bring any of the good tapes, but I think they're stellar selections. I love you for who you are, Sly says. We've heard this song five times already.

Miranda stands behind Josephine, who is much

taller, making a V above her head with tiny fingers. Miranda's come as Iowa. She packed herself in marshmallows colored with canary spray paint and green plastic trash bags rubber-banded to her arms for the husk. I told Miranda canary's all wrong for corn. Canary's a bird, I told Miranda. And then I found out it was her stepfather, Vern, who helped her pick out the paint. Vern, the guy who once told me that Miranda would be a real looker when she got a little older and then winked at me, his hand straying someplace below Miranda's back.

'But if anything was possible,' Josephine says squeezing the Honey Bear. A tear of honey wedges in the crease between her nose and cheek. She's looking right at me now. 'If *anything* was.'

Josephine likes the noise the Honey Bear makes, like people after they've been crying, she told me. I didn't understand. Because that means it's all over, she said, whatever it was that made them sad. I can't keep her away from the gluebirds at school either.

'I guess if anything was possible that would be it,' I say. She turns and, catching Miranda off guard, tells her '*See*,' and Miranda shuts her eyes tight. I ask, 'How's your nose?'

'I stubbed it on the screen door.'

I look closer. There's a little grid etched in blood just over her right nostril. 'I'm sorry,' I say.

'Why are you sorry? You didn't do anything.'

She gets that line from her mother. You can only be sorry for people if you've done them some harm, otherwise you're just patronizing them. 'Maybe I'm

14

sorry because I didn't teach you how to open a screen door.'

Miranda thinks this is very funny. Her laughter carries out over the lawn, where children run around waving American flags in miniature, a patriotic freeze tag. Winston, a quiet kid, stands on the periphery aiming the sprinkler key at the sky, which has become very still. It's obvious he doesn't like being dressed up as a giant spud. You can change if you want, I told him, put it back on before your mom picks you up. He shook his head. His mother wears industrial-strength perfume and calls him Winnie in front of the other kids, who don't let him forget about it. 'Oh, Winnie just adores playing with Mr Potato Head,' she told me over the phone this morning. I never dreamed she could be this diabolical.

'Where's your mom?' I ask Josephine. Now she's looking at the ground.

'Faye,' Josephine says. She doesn't call her mom Mom anymore.

'Where's your Faye?'

'I'm not sure,' she says. The frown ripples through her forehead. It's her mother's forehead; you could show movies on that thing.

'She's a big woman these days – like Texas,' I say. 'How could you lose her?'

She looks up. 'I thought Texas was flat.'

'What about the Pecos?' I say.

'What about them?'

Josephine will be in the sixth grade next year. God knows what grade her mother will be in. She's going on thirty-two and tells me, when I cup my ear over her great belly, that children are just erupted volcanos, lava waiting to harden. There's no point in saying anything when she gets like this, which seems to be often of late. Sometimes I wonder if Joey left her because of her mercurial temperament. On Valentine's Day he sent her a big box wrapped in expensive paper. I had just met Faye then; she had invited me over to have a talk about Josephine, who wasn't doing very well with her fractions. I can't ever remember seeing Faye so happy as when the delivery boy set that big box down in her living room. Kinked ribbon, heart-shaped card, the whole bit. But when she opened the box there was nothing in it except a cooking thermometer and a note from Joey that made her cry. I stayed with Faye until dawn. In bed she told me she had an unnatural fear of telephones, telephones that ring in the middle of the night. She spoke as if the rest of us feared them like black widow spiders. I don't ever call her after the sun goes down.

'That doesn't help your nose any,' I say to Josephine, who's rubbing her wound again. 'Unhand that Honey Bear.' I grab the bear from her and hold it over my head. Josephine looks troubled.

'She was in the bathtub when I left,' she says. 'I got a ride with Miranda in Vern's truck. Now give it back.' She leans me into the fence trying to get the Honey Bear.

'I'm the Statue of Liberty,' I say. 'This is the entrance to New York Harbor.' Josephine tickles my waist. 'So she's coming then?'

'You wish.'

'In what state?'

'I'm not supposed to tell.'

16

'Trust me, Josie, I'm your teacher.'

'Just give it back,' she says.

I drop the Honey Bear on the grass. Miranda snatches it up and dashes for the alley with Josephine in close pursuit, canary marshmallows scattering everywhere. The batteries on my ghetto blaster are running low – Sly just dropped a whole octave. I don't own an extension cord, but my brother, the other grownup I invited to the party, is supposed to bring one. As grownups go, he's not very reliable. Lately he's been trying to convince himself that women are figments of his baroque imagination, especially his ex-fiancée, but he has a hard time with Faye. She says 'Boo' a lot when he's around, waits in closets, stuff like that. Last week she answered the door with a tablecloth over her head, and my brother got mad. 'I'm only trying to make myself more imaginary,' Faye told him. 'Imaginary beings never say things like that,' my brother said. Then Faye pushed her stomach out, a hunchback in reverse, and made her face into a pizza dough with her hands. I told them they'd have to take it outside.

Lionel tugs on my Hawaiian shirt for the umpteenth time. He needs to know when we get to bust open the piñata; he brought a number 27 Louisville Slugger to use on it. I told him half an hour ago that we don't have a piñata, that the budget only allows for a piñata once a year, and that's on Cinco de Mayo.

'One good cut at that toro-cow,' he says, swinging the bat, 'and I'll sky them taffies all the way to Mexico.' Sly is practically subsonic now. A little bit

17

lower and he'll start a rockslide. 'You smoke dope?' Lionel asks. He's been talking to his brothers again. One of them's in jail for beating up his girl friend with a traffic flare. Lionel's eyes roll back in his head and he opens his mouth wide as if breathing for the last time. 'Teacher,' he says, his voice almost a breeze, 'if dope was a snake, would you have got bit?'

The sky is heavy, nearly dangling, when my brother finally shows up. He has his back to the setting sun as he walks toward me with his clarinet. Any good guy would be riding in the opposite direction. In the fifth grade my brother gave up the saxophone after a week because it was too heavy to carry to school. I think my mother secretly hoped he would give up music forever, because my father practiced arcane arpeggios in her sewing room for years and would never play 'Moon River' when she asked him to, even on their anniversary. Her dream faded when my brother took up a lighter instrument. He won't play 'Moon River' for her either.

There's a second when the ghetto blaster revives itself. Sly starts out from a growl: 'You don't need darkness to do what you think is right.' The fallen sun cuts around my brother, like air around a wing, and drives into my eyes. He's saying something in a loud, good-natured voice but I can't make out what it is, and then I remember it's my sight that's been disabled; my ears should be working perfectly.

The parents will be arriving soon to pick up their children in VW vans and Chevy Monzas and Gran Torinos and I'm much too drunk to deal with any of it. They'll be well along themselves, of course, a couple of scotches and a wine or two. Maybe even a tongue kiss in the family room, the kid away and all. But on the road home with the radio going and their son propped up in back, they wonder about my drinking, my affair with one of the mothers, whether maybe they should put him in a private school next year. Be a good Idaho, they say. Look out the window and be scared like us, but don't let it show – if we run out of gas, this car will go on night alone. The kid wants to say something. His mouth gets funny like a stroke victim's and Mommy shushes him before he has a chance to speak up. She turns on the dome light as if guilty for taking him to a horror movie she couldn't bear to leave. And he only wanted to say that Daddy closed the door on his safety belt; it's dragging on the bumpy street, sparks flying in the corners of their eyes, the clatter like the heartbeat they've grown so accustomed to these days.

My brother asks, 'What's the matter with your pupils?' He's opened the clarinet case on his lap. His hands are hidden from my view.

'Come on, they're great kids.'

'I meant the ones in your eyes,' he says. 'You shouldn't smoke marijuana by yourself. Everything becomes everything else.'

He knows that I haven't smoked marijuana since Faye, alone or otherwise. He's still fiddling around with something in the case. He sets the bell and the mouthpiece in the grass – maybe an earwig will crawl in there. I ask him if he believes in magic.

'No camera tricks,' he says. 'Everything you see is real, folks!' With a '*voilà*' and a wave of his hand

19

he produces the extension cord. 'It's ten feet long – do you think it'll reach?'

'Faye's coming over,' I say.

'Goody,' he says, 'we can tie her up with it. Pregnant hostages work the best.'

'I just want you to be social, that's all.'

'When haven't I been social?'

'When's the last time you saw Faye?'

My brother says he better start the burgers before it gets much darker. I show him where I keep the briquettes. 'By the way,' he tells me, 'Merry Flag Day.' His chuckling separates from his body as he disappears around the side of the house. He can't understand why I want to see a pregnant woman, except maybe that they have big charlies. 'Get a Betty who's disposable,' he's told me. 'You know, a Lady Schick.'

But what he doesn't realize is that I save everything – newspapers, milk cartons, chicken-pot-pie tins. They're stacked up under the house with the firewood. Someday I'll use them in Art Period.

Lionel and his friend Carl are shouting 'Fore' and throwing glow-in-the-dark Frisbees over the other children, who, for the most part, seem dazed, probably from hunger. I grab Lionel by the jersey – he's in a baseball uniform for some reason – and ask him not very politely what the hell he thinks he's doing. Lionel gets scared for a second.

'Frisbee golf, Mr Vanvoort. Wanna play?' He offers me the luminous disk. 'It's best to shoot for something you can't see.'

I shake my head no and, feeling drained, glance

20

around the yard for a good place to lean. Miranda and Josephine are having an argument about insects.

'Bugs don't kill themselves,' Josephine says. 'How would they do it, jump off a building?'

Miranda gestures to the porch light, where a bunch of dead moths have accumulated. I could intercede here, be teacherlike and tell them that moths navigate by the moon and that they're fooled by artificial light and probably never realize the difference. Is being quixotic the same as being suicidal? I'm tempted to ask Josephine, but I know she would think I was teasing her and I would be. Faye doesn't like me teasing Josephine because she says I'm an authority figure and authority figures should always be sincere. She *really* doesn't like it because Joey teases Josephine a lot and Faye likes to think that I don't remind her of Joey even though I do.

My brother is afraid I might do the Right Thing. I've pointed out that it's not my child Faye's carrying, and besides for the Right Thing it has to be her first kid, her first marriage, at least that's how I've always understood it. At any rate, I tried proposing on April Fool's Day, just to see how Faye would react. She got real nervous and told me I was kidding, stop kidding, she said. But you could tell she thought I was serious. And the problem is I'm not sure if I *was* serious, and if I was, I'm not sure how she was reacting. If I'd waited a little longer before I said April Fool's I might've found out, but I got afraid of my own joke – I didn't want to know – and Josephine walked in right after I said it, waving one of those pocket-size electric fans. After Faye was through yelling at Josephine, the subject of marriage didn't come up again.

We sit around the fire, all pretty much wasted. None of us has the energy to cope with inertia so the party goes on and on. Vern's here now, smelling of Old Spice and wearing a bolo tie with a pair of snake-eye dice set in acrylic. Above the coals my brother waits. He has grilled several night-flying insects already, mashing them down with the spatula until their wings are forced through the hot metal into the red abyss. Lionel's sitting Indian-style with his Frisbee in his lap – it isn't glowing anymore. His mother said she would be here at seven-thirty to pick him up, but that was hours ago and no one answers when I call his house. Josephine and Miranda sit a little way back from the fire telling knock-knock jokes in the dark. The rest of the offspring have been retrieved. A couple of the parents brought me gifts supposedly from their children: a tie clasp in the shape of a paper clip, a coffee mug that says World's Greatest Teacher on it. Some of the parents hoped that I'd draw their next-in-lines in the big raffle in September. Some of the parents took away their children quietly.

And then Faye came, beautiful Faye, through a break in the back fence, with her sarong pulled up over her shins like a rice worker, like a Taiwanese wading in the paddies. I told her I'd do her leeches with a Spanish cigarette. She didn't know what I was talking about, but she didn't get that perplexed look either, which means she's probably in a good mood. I didn't ask her why she was so late. She brought a pineapple and a fifth of Bacardi dark, unopened. She says she's Puerto Rico.

This evening I have proposed several times to Faye. I have found her in places: the alley, with her back to me, her hair pulled above her white neck, a barrette clenched in her teeth; my kitchen, eating a cold hot dog and staring over my shoulder at the clock, asking me softly, 'What time do you think it is?'; my bathroom, urinating with the door partly open the way my mother always did until we got older and my father made her shut it. Ah, Faye, beautiful Faye.

My brother has abandoned his place by the fire. He's trying to attach the extension cord to the ghetto blaster but it's caught on something and he can't get it loose. Instead of doing the easy thing and moving the ghetto blaster a little closer, he jerks spasmodically on the cord, his head almost colliding with Faye's belly after each pull. Faye is sprawled out on the grass. I don't think she and my brother have said two words to each other the entire night. Earlier, he tried to coax the kids up the alley with his clarinet, but they wouldn't go for it.

Finally my brother gets exasperated and throws the extension cord as far as he can, which isn't very far. He turns to me as if frustration jogged his memory. He says, 'Do you remember when I was graduating from college and that weird thing happened in the balcony?'

I wasn't at his graduation. I was running rivers that summer in the Gold Country and I had left the week before. But my brother's face is lit up all around the edges, his eyes lost in the shadow of his brow. I don't have the heart to tell him I wasn't there, so I just nod along.

'It was right after they graduated the business majors,' he says. 'I remember because when they announced it over the PA they all cheered and threw Monopoly money in the air.'

He looks at me funny and smiles. I think he remembers that I wasn't at his graduation.

'But right after that,' he says, 'these firecrackers or gunshots or something go off in the balcony, you know, like Ford's Theater, and this guy Franklin Somethingorother stands up with one of those battery-operated microphones. You remember Franklin. He was the guy who claimed he regularly communicated with the Saucer People, remember? He used to hand out Jesus pamphlets by the wuddayacallit – you know, it had that funny sound, almost Eskimo – kiosk, that's it. He used to hand out Jesus pamphlets by the kiosk with his wife and little baby.'

I do remember him now. He got arrested one time for putting 'Jesus Coming Soon' on the marquee at the little revival house downtown.

'So anyway,' my brother says, 'Franklin makes sure he has everybody's attention and then he starts reading off this three-by-five, a prepared statement, for chrissakes. It's so weird. "How do you make a baby float?" he says. I swear, right off the card. Then he looks around the hall to see if anyone's got the answer – of course nobody does – so he answers his own question. "You fill him with influence," he says. I remember it clear as day. Some things just stick in your head, like the first verse of Good King Wenceslaus we had to learn for the Christmas show in third grade.'

I can't even remember the melody to that song.

'We read about it in the paper the next day,' my brother says. 'He took his kid out to the Mad River and pushed him down until he wouldn't come up anymore. We were all pretty hung over. The folks were having their argument about toast.'

Faye is up and screaming at my brother. 'People don't talk like that,' she says. She pushes the barbecue over but misses him easily, and then stalks off into the darkness. The coals are all over the lawn.

Nobody says anything for a while. Then Vern clears his throat and tells me that he better get Miranda home, it's getting past her bedtime. Lionel asks Vern if maybe he could catch a ride and then looks at me earnestly. 'I know where she hides the house key,' he says. I don't believe him for a second, but I'm too tired to argue. Vern says, 'Sure, I'll give you a lift.'

I hug Miranda, tell her I'll miss her, and she kisses me on the cheek when I stoop over. I tell Lionel to give me some skin, and right after I say it I realize that it's not the phrase anymore. Lionel is grinning. He fully comprehends my awkwardness. He reaches out and gives me a straight handshake.

'Mutate or die,' he says laughing, 'mutate or die.'

Vern takes Miranda by the hand and guides her to the truck. Lionel is right behind them, shaking his head and walking his stilted walk. He forgot his mother's tapes.

I feel something cool on the backs of my legs and turn to find Josephine hosing down the coals in her

wilted hive suit. A Band-Aid dangles from the
bridge of her nose.

'You always wanted to be a fireman, didn't you,
Josie?'

'Just tonight,' she says.

'You know what I want to be when I grow up?'

She shrugs.

'Anything,' I say, 'anything at all.'

I stagger barefoot over slugs and broken water
balloons and little flags, even a grounded kite,
on my way to find Faye. My first clue is her sniffling,
like the Honey Bear, and when I call out, 'Faye, is
that you?' she says, 'No.' She's sitting against a
fence post in the corner of the yard. I ask, 'Is everything all right here?'

'You say that like a waiter.' Her voice is cracked
with sobs.

'Maybe I should ask you if you'd like a slice of
pecan pie.' I can't see her face – my eyes haven't
adjusted to the dark yet. Last week somebody shot
out the street lamp with a BB gun.

After a while she says, 'I'm seven years older
than you are, seven more candles on my cake for
the rest of our lives. I have two children, or one
plus, and your brother's an asshole.' She pauses.
'Jesus, I don't want to be like this.'

I move closer, but I can't really see her yet, just
an image like an X-ray, patches of light on a sheet of
black. I imagine Lionel at home now, gliding
through his bedroom window as easy as a cat, and
it makes me feel good in an odd way, maybe
because I know he wouldn't think twice about doing

it. There's this weird feeling I get when I have to break into my own house, this anxiety that a stranger will see me and call the police. That's when I panic, break a window, anything to get inside. It's funny to think that a burglar would feel the same way, that the only difference between you and him is that you know you live there and he knows he doesn't.

'Faye?' I ask, out of breath, though I can't say why. 'Tell me that you'll love me forever and I promise I won't see you anymore.'

She pushes back my hair with her hand, letting it fall down over my eyes.

'I'll love you forever,' she says.

THE PAINTER

Hurst had never liked the ring of Arabelle's telephone. It was low and unmelodious, the way phones on daytime movies sound when the coffee-mug host dials the number on a postcard drawn scrupulously at random. He was sitting cross-legged on a mattress in his living room with the receiver held a small distance from his ear. He couldn't understand why she didn't answer; it was winter now and it was her habit during the cold months to stay in bed until three or four on Saturday afternoons reading some long-winded Russian novel. She didn't believe in reading translations. She had told him this at least five times in the year that he'd known her.

He switched the receiver to his other ear and unzipped his sweat shirt. He had only the one question, which of course involved the painting, and then he would leave her alone. A simple question. A question anyone with half a brain might ask. The painting was leaning against the wall in front of him, next to his sleeping cat and some jelly beans in a crystal brandy snifter. The rest of his belongings had been moved to his parents' house in Los Angeles. He reached over and picked up the brandy snifter

29

and began swirling it gently as though it contained Courvoisier, or one of those expensive liqueurs that Arabelle was always sipping. The jelly beans had been the realtor's idea, to sweeten the deal, as she'd put it, but so far no offers had been tendered. Maybe it was because he'd eaten all the good flavors, Hurst thought, the licorice and pineapple and cherry. Only the pinks and purples remained, flavors he was certain didn't exist in the natural world. 'The natural world,' he said into the phone. It was Arabelle's term. He put a handful of jelly beans in his mouth and chewed them thoroughly but did not swallow. The hell with the natural world, he thought.

The painting was an impressionistic rendering of Jell-O salads. Five Jell-O salads in a lit deli case. Hurst had never heard of the guy who painted it, but Arabelle had called the artist a lesser Thiebaud. Hurst had never heard of this guy Thiebaud either. He set the phone down on the hardwood floor – he thought he could still hear the ringing – and stared at the painting with as blank an expression as he could muster. He pretended he was viewing the painting in a gallery, as though it were roped off and a severe-looking man with an earplug and red blazer were standing next to it. He put another handful of jelly beans in his mouth and swallowed this time without chewing. He looked at the phone and then looked back at the painting.

'BFD,' he said.

Arabelle had practically had an orgasm when she first saw the painting in a conference room where they worked. Where *she* worked, Hurst reminded himself. He had been fired after he refused to give the painting back. It had fit easily into his gym bag, so easily that he wondered at the time why he had never stolen anything before. He supposed now that it had something obliquely to do with Arabelle's reaction – she had been dazzlingly unimpressed when he unveiled the painting in her apartment, the last in a series of unimpressions, and he was convinced that she had been the one who turned him in. The last time he asked her about this, she threatened to change her phone number. It didn't seem like such a tough question to Hurst.

The cat jumped up and scrabbled on the hardwood, like a cat in a cartoon, before gaining enough traction to flee the room; someone was knocking on the door. Hurst draped his sweat shirt over the painting and waited for a second knocking. When none came, he tiptoed quietly to the threshold and peered out the little stained-glass window in the door. He couldn't see anyone, but he hadn't heard footsteps going back down the stairs. He listened intently and thought he heard someone gasping. Then he heard nothing.

After a time, a young woman's voice said, 'I know you're in there.'

Hurst remained silent.

'Are you a deaf mute?' she asked, and when Hurst again failed to respond, she began gently to twist the doorknob, which Hurst grasped and countertwisted with equal force. This went on for several seconds before Hurst, in a panic, engaged the deadbolt. He did not consider himself an impulsive person and rarely opened the door to strangers.

'I saw you sitting in your Camaro a while ago,' the

young woman said. 'You have bad posture and a kind face.' She laughed a little laugh and then coughed. A little laugh for a little person, Hurst decided. Arabelle was tall and thin and claimed people were always approaching her for modeling jobs. Right, Hurst said under his breath, that's why you're a research librarian.

'I would've given you a balloon,' the young woman continued, 'but I didn't have any at the time. You looked like you could've used a balloon right then.' Her voice trailed off as though she had turned away, and Hurst wondered if she was giving up.

'Or really anything that floats,' she said at her original volume.

Hurst looked at the phone.

'Really I didn't mean that about your posture. Really what I meant is that you looked so pained, all slumped over the wheel like that. I've never seen anybody slumped over the wheel like that. Not anybody who was still alive.'

There was a pause and then Hurst heard a rustling noise at the base of the door. He watched as a business card slid over the weather stripping. He knelt and picked it up. The card had been hand-typed. It said: 'M. LISA.'

'I don't blame you for taking precautions,' the young woman said quietly – it was as if she were telling Hurst that his fly was undone. 'Curt never let me open the door for anyone. He always felt a certain animosity toward strangers, though I could never say I really understood it. I think he had suspicions about his own character is what I think.'

'What are you selling?' Hurst blurted out and

immediately felt, by virtue of his speaking, that he'd been suckered into something. 'My house is already insulated and I don't wear makeup.'

'How funny,' the young woman said flatly. 'I'm selling the future, Mr Hurst, what everybody needs. It's my own future, of course, but that doesn't mean it has no bearing on your own.' The little laugh surfaced again from behind the door. 'It's kind of involved,' she said. 'Plus it's very cold out here.' She paused. 'Mr Hurst.'

He was still young enough to be surprised when people addressed him as Mr. He wasn't sure that he liked it.

'There's no one here by that name,' Hurst said and stood back from the door. It had occurred to him that this whole thing was probably a ruse, that really this person wanted to serve him with a subpoena. The painting meant a lot of things to a lot of people, Hurst thought, though he didn't consider himself one of them. 'What makes you think my name is Hurst?'

'You're on my list,' she said convincingly. 'That's the way the world operates: you're on my list, I'm on somebody else's.' He heard her strike a match and then put it out with her shoe. He decided she must be wearing high heels, though he had no logical basis for his decision. 'Of course, everyone's on the master list,' she said. 'Only nobody has it. Not even God or the phone company.'

Hurst leaned his forehead against the door. The wood was cold. 'I would like you to please leave me alone now,' he said. 'I'm unemployed and what little money I've saved is being squandered on mortgage

33

payments until I can sell this house. I've been living on peanut butter and jelly beans for the last three days and my cat's been eating insects and small rodents. My cat has always been afraid to go outside until now. You might say his behavior is adaptive.'

'Adaptive,' he repeated to himself – it was another one of Arabelle's words. He had meant to sound dramatic, but now he realized that what he had just told this stranger was true. Hurst suddenly saw himself as a desperate man.

'No pain, no gain,' the young woman said matter-of-factly. 'That was always Curt's philosophy, right up through the arraignment.' She laughed and coughed at the same time. 'My motto goes slightly different – "no pain, no pain." '

He wanted to ask her about his posture, if he was really slouching toward a premature death. He put his hand on the deadbolt latch and squeezed it.

'You can keep my card,' she said. 'I wrote my number on the back. Give me a call sometime.' She gave the doorknob a last twist. 'I might not pass this way again.'

He waited for her footsteps on the stairs. He waited for fifteen minutes. He couldn't hear anything and he wondered if, in his state of desperation, he might have missed her leaving. He walked through the rooms of the house with his hand on the wall at all times, as though he were feeling his way out of a cave. It was late afternoon and the winter sun shining through the skylight made him feel bleached and melancholy. In the kitchen, he called to himself, listening to the flat sound of his own

voice. He returned to the living room and undraped
the painting, tossing his sweat shirt onto the
mattress. He picked the phone up off the floor. It
was still ringing. He set it back down again.

Eventually he opened the door.

She was sitting on the porch eating a submarine
sandwich. He supposed she looked the way he
thought she would, though she was wearing a gray
corduroy skirt and a gray-and-white-plaid blouse,
clothes he associated with parochial school. And
she had on a pair of deck shoes, not the high red
pumps he'd imagined. There was a bright orange
balloon the size of a basketball in her lap. She didn't
look a thing like Arabelle.

'Excellent,' she said to herself, though she was
looking directly at Hurst. She stood up and tossed
the butt of her sandwich into the street below. They
both watched as it rolled up against the far curb
and fell open, exposing the pink lunchmeat inside.
Hurst wondered if his cat would eat it later.

'This is for you,' she said and handed him the
balloon. 'Orange is my favorite color. They say the
best presents are the ones you'd give yourself.'

Hurst thought he would never give anyone a
balloon, especially himself. He was holding it out
from his body as though it might indelibly mark him.

'Is it all right if I come in?' she asked.

Hurst nodded.

'You'd better put that in some water,' she said
thunking the balloon with her finger. Then she
laughed and Hurst realized she was making a joke.
The laugh seemed bigger now. Hurst decided it was
the acoustics of an empty house.

'No furniture,' she said, surveying the room. 'I guess you had to hock that.'

'It's in storage,' he said, aware now that he was slouching. He threw his shoulders back and stood up straighter.

'I never did like warehouses,' she said. 'They're always so drafty. It's not something you could explain with science, either.' She stood her ground, smiling and rubbing her bare arms with her hands. 'It's at the spiritual level,' she said.

Hurst found himself staring – she was older than she dressed. She could have been twenty-two or twenty-three. 'The door,' he said apologetically and turned to shut it.

'You're pretty young to own your own house,' she said. She was looking at the painting. 'You live here by yourself?'

'By choice,' Hurst said.

'I guess there's no point in discussing fate – since it's going to happen anyway, I mean.' She took a pack of cigarettes out of a pocket in her skirt. 'Is smoking allowed?'

He smiled and felt as though he were having his picture taken. He wished she would just hand him the subpoena and get it over with. 'I took the batteries out of the smoke detector last week,' he said. 'You shouldn't have any problem.'

'You knew I was coming, then,' she said and looked him in the eye. Then she laughed. 'Your phone's off the hook, know that?' She lit her cigarette and blew out the match. 'No wonder I kept getting a busy signal.'

Hurst waited for the laugh. Instead, she glanced

about the room another time. 'Do you have some-where to put this?' she said, holding out the match.

He set the balloon on the mattress and picked up the brandy snifter. 'Here,' he said.

'Oh, I couldn't spoil your jelly beans.'

'They were spoiled already.'

She seemed to be blushing, which took Hurst completely off guard. 'Do you mind if I have a few?' she asked. 'Pink was always my favorite flavor. They're grapefruit, you know. Pink grapefruit, like from Florida. That's really the purpose of this visit.' She managed to scoop up a handful with the match still in her hand. 'Florida, I mean.'

She smiled and Hurst, without smiling back, withdrew the brandy snifter. Then he saw that she was still holding the match. He politely took it out of her hand and put it in the pocket of his sweat pants. He was trying to connect Florida to the painting, but he kept thinking about his grandmother instead. She had been dying in Miami for years now, though she always managed to send him a box of candied ginger at Christmas. It had always been a great source of anxiety for Hurst, especially since he hated candied ginger.

'Florida?' he said finally and realized he was slouching again. He leaned himself against the wall, trying to appear casual. He envisioned him-self with a drink in his hand and felt more at ease. Then he remembered the jelly beans.

'Florida,' she said, as though her inflection had transformed his question into an answer. She winked at him and withdrew a folded sheet of paper from her skirt. He thought it must be the subpoena, but when he looked closer he saw that it was a pane of advertising stamps.

'I'm a participant in the Youth America program,' she said, 'one of five thousand young people across the nation who are selling magazines in hopes of fulfilling a dream.' Her voice was singsongy now. 'That dream is Orlando, Florida, Mr Hurst. The top five sellers win an all-expenses trip to Disney World, which includes a behind-the-scenes look at the facility and a week's lodging in nearby Everglades National Park.' She caught her breath by inhaling her cigarette. 'And after that nobody says I have to leave.' The smoke was still coming out of her mouth. She winked at him again.

'My name isn't Hurst,' Hurst said. 'And you know I don't have any money.'

She looked at him without acknowledging his presence in the room. It was as though she were considering one of twenty canned responses to the plea of bankruptcy. At last she said, 'What do you call yourself then?' and tapped her cigarette ash into the brandy snifter in Hurst's hand.

'Thiebaud,' he said, 'Wayne Thiebaud.' He carefully gauged her reaction. She didn't seem to have any. 'I'm a painter,' he said.

She took a long drag, letting the smoke out through her nose. 'My name's Lisa.'

He expected her to offer him her hand. She didn't. 'What's the M stand for?' he asked.

'Hmm?'

'On your card.' He reached into his pocket and brought out the crumpled card. She unfolded it in his hand and read it, as she might a fortune from a cookie.

'Moaner,' she said. 'Moaner Lisa – Curt gave me that name.' She was blushing again. 'They say Mona Lisa had a mouth disease, that's why she smiled so funny.'

She took a short, studied drag on her cigarette. 'So you're an unemployed painter. What do you paint—' she interrupted herself with another drag – 'when you're employed?'

'Jell-O,' he said.

'I didn't know Jell-O had to be painted.' She tossed the rest of her cigarette into the brandy snifter. 'I thought it just came out that way.'

'I'm an artist,' Hurst said and stepped over to the painting. 'Jell-O is my subject. I paint pictures of Jell-O.'

She leaned over and squinted at the painting, which was mostly concealed by shadow. 'Oh, is that what that is. I didn't know people still painted *things*. All the new art I've seen looks like one big brain dump.' She stepped closer and Hurst switched on the overhead light. 'Oh yeah,' she said. 'That's spiffy the way you drew in those little marshmallows. And is that a raisin?' She pointed to a dark spot in a lime Jell-O.

'No,' Hurst said. 'That's a rat pellet. I started out as a social realist.'

'I'd rather think of it as a raisin,' she said and stood up. She was still squinting, only now she was looking at Hurst. 'How come your picture's signed "Morrison"?'

Without flinching, Hurst set the brandy snifter on the floor. 'That's my brush name,' he said. 'Like a pen name for a writer – Mark Twain, for example.'

She sat down on the mattress. 'I painted a garage door once. With spray paint. I don't think the owner was too happy about it.' She laughed and crossed her legs. 'You must be pretty good if you make your living at it.'

'I have too many imitators here,' he said. He was smiling now, impressed with his own answers. When he realized she was staring at him, he shaped his mouth into a grimace. 'I'm thinking about moving to Paris.'

'Gay Paree,' she said. She looked as if she had just remembered leaving something expensive in a locker there. 'When were you thinking about traveling?' She lay back on the mattress with her head resting against the balloon. 'I sound like an airline reservationist.'

'As soon as I sell this house,' Hurst said.

'That could take weeks,' she said, and sat back up again. She was smiling broadly now whereas Hurst had taken on an actual grimace. 'The reason I ask is because our program has two avenues for sponsorship. I've already discussed the first, a more or less financial arrangement, but the second—' she poked him in the shin and looked up at his face, which was rapidly clouding – 'the second involves a living arrangement. It's a long, steep road to adulthood, as I'm sure you realize, Mr Thiebaud, but Youth America believes that road can be made more gradual with the help of responsible members from the community. Experience is the most valuable commodity, and I'd only be walking in your shoes for a week or so – feed your cat, use your shower, drive your car – and afterward you'd have that inner glow that comes with any sponsorship, Mr Thiebaud, be it spiritual or material.'

'I don't know,' Hurst said and stared at the phone again – he was trying to determine if it was still ringing. He sat down on the mattress without a clue and lifted the receiver off the floor.

'You could paint me,' she said, looking up at the ceiling, and it was as though nothing were there, as though night had already fallen and she were lying in a pasture watching the moon. 'You could paint *me*.'

'Yes,' he said, listening to his own voice echo in the receiver. 'Yes.'

And of course Arabelle's phone was still ringing, though he was surprised to hear that it was. He listened to it for a long time, letting its drone lull him into a kind of hypnosis. He wondered if there was an established limit for rings, if at some point an operator would break in and tell you that the person you were trying to reach was simply not home. He knew deep down that no such boundary existed, but he wanted to believe that one did.

He looked over at the woman lying on his bed. She was breathing slowly and steadily, and when he asked, 'What should we do?' her silence told him she was sleeping. He laid the receiver back in its cradle and stood above her, imagining himself to be her soul. She was pretty in a cherubic way – rounded cheeks, short broad nose – and beneath her lower lip was a scar that caused her mouth to curl up on one side: it was the beginning of a smile.

He knelt and picked up a fitted sheet that was wadded up by her ankles and without a sound opened it and began to drape it over her body. But he suddenly changed course and spread the sheet out on the floor next to her, weighting the perimeter with jelly beans so that it made a smooth surface against the wood. Then he worked his hand delicately into her skirt pocket, bringing out the book of matches, and just as delicately walked to the door and opened it.

A gust of cold wind moved his hair back over his head, but he didn't stop to put on his sweat shirt or his shoes. It was in the last stages of dusk now, that point when you can actually watch the world change colors, when light passes so quickly you could swear it makes a sound. From the porch Hurst thought he could still see what was left of her sandwich lying in the gutter across the street, but when he reached the base of the stairs he couldn't make it out anymore, only the little white square on the curb where the street number had been painted with a stencil. He walked out across his lawn, the cold earth seeping up through his socks, and pulled out the For Sale sign in one, deliberate try. Then he leaned the sign against the side of the house and entered the garage. It was pitch black inside, but he made his way without stumbling to a cabinet at the back. He opened the doors and lit a match and was pleased to see that it was right where he remembered, on top of a little stack of newspapers. It had come with the house, though he'd never used it – a can of white latex paint.

LIGHTHOUSE

On the occasion of our goodbye, Ruth told me, 'Freeman, you're a free man.' That was six months ago at the Amtrak station in Grants Pass where we were riding out the last, cloudy moments of Happy Hour with a pitcher of wine margaritas. I'd just given Ruth a deck of those porno playing cards, only with men on the backs instead of women, and I fanned them out in front of her, wearing this cat's grin, like a little kid who thinks he's putting one over on his mother. 'Ruth,' I said in my coolest voice, 'pick a stud, any stud.' And then we both started to laugh because we'd decided only that morning that our separation didn't have to be permanent, and we kept on laughing until a couple in the next booth turned around and looked at us, as if they'd missed the funniest joke in the world.

I remember from Psychology that crazy people always laugh at the wrong times, in which case Ruth and I were certifiable. We laughed the first time we made love, Ruth's first ever, in my camper shell with the dome light on, and later we laughed after I rolled the camper near Bridgeport and we wound up wading the

Truckee River in the middle of the night to call out Triple A.

So I guess it's consistent that we left each other laughing, as though everything was set between us from that day on. I was a senior in college when I first met Ruth, and I was still a senior three years later when we moved into a little duplex out in the Bottoms. It was a stormy nine months to be sure, though I never cheated on Ruth in that time and I *had* two-timed her in the past. Through all of it, we were still together at our graduation and, as Ruth put it, there was nowhere else but marriage after that. Marriage or a little time off.

All of which is told nicely in Ruth's letter, dated the Fourth of July, that Vicki Whitehorse is reading out loud without my permission. It's Christmas Eve now and I'm living in a hotel, the Wild Deuce, in a little desert town called Lighthouse, Nevada, which is named after the state monument where Vicki and I work as tour guides. Vicki can't officially be a guide since she doesn't have a college degree, but I let her swap places with me on every other tour and I work the register in the curios shop. It was the one job the Park Service had to offer me out of school, a 'seasonal' position, and I took it with the idea that I could tolerate anything for six months, though I realize now what a long time that can be. Vicki's the only woman I've been alone with since I got here, and she doesn't really count because she's married. But I figure we're in the same boat anyway, what with her husband, Bill, staking mercury in the Stillwater Mountains for most of the last two years, and me dancing the slow limbo with Ruth Anne Chaney. Ruth lives with her widowed mother in Phoenix now where she's following her ambition as an elementary school teacher.

'So what do the X's and Y's mean again?' Vicki asks me in her normal voice. She always tries to impersonate Ruth when she reads Ruth's letters out loud, even though she's never met Ruth or even heard her talk. The effect is like one of Vicki's tours – so false it's a type of sincere. 'Aren't they some kind of signal or something?'

'Instead of X's and O's,' I say, but Vicki does her confused act. She thinks it's good for me to have to explain this next part. 'Because chromosomes are a lot deeper than hugs and kisses. We met in Biology, remember?'

Vicki takes a slug out of my Thermos – she has it full of Snap-E-Tom and mostly Everclear – and leans back against the windowsill, smiling profusely. She's wearing a Santa Claus hat and cowboy boots and her backless teal-green dress, the dress that shows off her 'noticeable' spine as she refers to it. According to Vicki, this is her most striking feature, though I give the nod to her 'noticeable' legs. They're quite remarkable for a woman her age, which I guess is in her forties.

'She's wild about you,' Vicki says, but her voice goes mainly in the Thermos. 'Who isn't wild about video stars?'

'Ruth,' I say and lean back on my campstool. I sent her a videotape of myself that I made at the Radio Shack in Lake Tahoe. The manager was reluctant to do it at first – he was a young guy, about Ruth's age – but when I told him it was for my girl friend, he said, 'Sure, why not?' I had on my graduation suit and the skinny tie that Ruth had sent me for my birthday and I started with a speech about our forthcoming reunion and then broke into 'Singin' in the Rain' plus the little dance step that goes with it, which is no mean feat in a pair of Red Wings. Ruth's next and last correspondence came a month later – one of those post-office postcards that don't have pictures – and all it mentioned was this bachelorette party she'd been to the night before where everyone put on wedding veils and bobbed for little chocolate penises in a bucket of milk.

'Ruth didn't know how to have a good time until she met you,' Vicki says.

'That's all she gives me credit for.'

'Pee-shaw,' Vicki says and puts Ruth's letter back in the shoebox where she found it. She's staring at me like I should know what she's thinking, which, of course, I don't.

'You didn't read the PS this time,' I say, where Ruth claims she'll meet me at the lighthouse at midnight Christmas Eve. Vicki's afraid to read that part because she doesn't want to get my hopes up, or at least any specific hopes. I haven't told her that I've got Ruth's present in the back of my camper. It's a ring that I bought in a pawnshop in Reno, like the one Ruth always said I'd buy her at Kent Hartley's when we got married, with a diamond that you Kent Hartley see. I kept the receipt just in case, though. It's tucked in the visor on the driver's side with the vehicle registration and a swizzle stick I got in an ad for the Mustang Ranch.

'PS I love you,' Vicki sings in her best Elvis vibrato. The setting sun, flattened against the windowsill behind her, casts a purplish light over her broad, rippled forehead. It was the Beatles who recorded 'PS I Love You', but I don't have it in me to tell her just now.

'Don't you know "Heartbreak Hotel"?' I ask.

'I don't do requests,' she says. 'Not anymore.' Vicki's brow tightens and she sits up, her Santa Claus hat pushed back on her head like a Stetson. 'Wasn't that in a movie?' she says.

'What?'

' "I don't do requests anymore." ' I'm pretty sure Sterling Hayden said it in one of those RKO pictures. You know, where that little radio tower gives off sparks at the beginning.'

'Everything you say is from a movie,' I tell her. And it's true. Especially movies where the characters say one thing and mean another. Bogart, Bacall, Bette Davis. But she also loves Westerns – every time they show a guy in a loincloth, she yells, 'My people,' as if Whitehorse is her maiden name and she's the one who's three-quarters Hoopa Indian. It really used to bother me, all of Vicki's posing, but now I think it's sweet. Ruth says you can't work with a person for any length of time without becoming attracted to them, and I suspect that she's right. I only wish there weren't so many men working at her grade school.

'The hills are alive with the sound of music,' Vicki says. 'What are we doing in your hotel room?'

'You were trying to cheer me up,' I say. 'What you've been trying to do for the last six months.'

'I can't cheer you up,' she says. 'You won't take my advice.' She sits back down again looking exasperated. 'So why should I give it to you?'

'So I'll know what *not* to do,' I say and wait a beat before I laugh. Vicki isn't laughing though, at least not visibly. She spent most of November trying to set me up with the woman who cashes chips in the hotel casino. I gambled there every morning for a while, buying steak and eggs if I won, fasting if I lost, and Carmen, who doubles as the desk clerk, used to wish me luck and wink at me. Vicki had it on good authority that Carmen thought I was hot stuff, but when I finally asked her out, she acted as though I was a perfect stranger.

I never did trust people who wink.

'It's your turn to do the cheering up,' Vicki says. 'Us mercury widows are a melancholy breed.'

'Sure,' I say. 'Tell me what to tell you.'

She smiles. 'Why don't you compare me favorably to one of your old girl friends? Somebody you slept with without thinking. Somebody before Ruth.'

'You need to get out of this place,' I say, and like most of my advice it's really directed toward me. I've never met anyone like Vicki before, for better or worse, though I'm sure Vicki is trying to get me to say it in a nicer way than that. We've been living each other's lives vicariously for so long now that we have to generate some new material. Either that or keep driving on fumes.

'Where should I go?' Vicki asks, more of herself than of me. 'Someplace with a decent rainfall, I guess. Florida maybe. Or the Islands.' She cranes her head toward mine, giving me these soft, brown doe eyes. 'And what about Billy?'

'You don't need a Billy,' I say and turn my head. I'm thinking about Ruth again, about the weird little moment when we first kissed each other, and I don't want to project her face onto Vicki's. Nothing scares me more than to think that lovers are interchangeable or, at least, that I might not be able to tell the difference.

'I don't need a man to tell me I don't need a man,' Vicki says. 'That's for damn sure.'

'No, you don't,' I say. I turn back to see what Vicki's expression is, but the twilight has slunk down to her chest now, leaving her face behind in the shadows.

'What do you see?' Vicki asks me.

'Mostly you.'

The last glint of sun exposes the dust fluttering in the space between us, and it makes the room seem smaller and filled with too many things. I stand up and excuse myself, feeling claustrophobic, and tell Vicki that I have to use the bathroom, which is a lie.

In the hall, Maybelline is standing over the ice machine smoking a cigarette and listening to someone on the pay phone. She's got her New Testament under her arm as usual, a habit that for the longest time kept me from guessing she was a hooker, one of the three who live at the Wild Deuce.

They drive up here from Oakland in the off season and leave again before it gets too hot, and every one of them will tell you when they're not in uniform that they're here to clear up some unnamed health condition. I can't imagine who their clientele is –

cowboys, I guess, or salesmen on their way to Reno, or maybe even park rangers like me, drunk and lonely and far away from home. That was something Ruth was always curious about, whether I'd ever bought sex from a whore. And whenever I told her that I hadn't, she'd poke me in the ribs and say, 'Oh, come on,' as though I was keeping a secret that all boys shared. My friend Danny got a hand job in the parking lot behind a strip joint once, but that's the only guy I ever knew who paid for anything, and even that was on a dare.

'You'll feel better soon,' Maybelline says quietly into the receiver. 'Pour yourself an eggnog and turn on the TV.' She sees me out of the corner of her eye and smiles shyly. I'm always embarrassed when I run into her because I think that she might talk about her work, though I have no real reason to think so – I wouldn't be caught dead discussing tours with anyone except Vicki.

'I know,' Maybelline says, running a painted fingernail along the metal phone cord, 'I know. God wants us all to have a merry Christmas.' She gently puts the receiver back in its cradle and turns around to face me. 'The holidays,' she says, shaking her head. 'They put a lot of people in a blue funk.'

'I've heard that,' I say. Maybelline's not wearing any makeup and the difference is startling. Her face reflects the dim light in the hallway much better now and it makes her seem younger, though not as young as me. 'I need to use the phone,' I tell her.

'Oh, I'm sorry,' she says, 'I didn't mean to get in your way.' She picks up her Bible from the ice machine and steps back a few feet. 'You're probably

50

going to call family, aren't you? Or maybe your sweetheart.'

'If I can get her at home,' I say. The hum of the ice machine is just loud enough to deflect the tenor of our voices and it makes me feel like I've been talking in this hallway for a long time.

'She will be,' Maybelline says. 'And if she's not then you can be sure the Lord's always home.'

'Thank you.' I've never been what you'd call a religious person, but I appreciate a kind gesture.

'You're welcome,' Maybelline says. She stares at me for a long time and then smiles to herself as though she's seen what she wanted to see. 'And if the Lord's line is busy, I'm in room 204,' she says. 'She put all of us on this earth to perform Her services. If you can't find God, find the next best thing.' She turns and struts down the hallway without seeming deliberate and quietly enters 204. I can see her shadow underneath the door for a long time before she steps back farther into the room.

I have change enough for a three-minute call to Phoenix. Ruth should've left by now if she's going to make it by twelve, but she's never been on time in her life and I figure I should go over the directions once more since I gave them to her a long time ago. I dial the number direct, but the connection doesn't go through and I can hear a hundred other callers saying hello, but without getting any response. It makes me wonder if each of them can hear my voice, and if it sounds as desperate and friendless. On the next call, I have the operator dial for me and when it finally rings another operator answers and says that Ruth's number's been changed.

51

'Will you connect me, please? I'm on a pay phone.'

'Yes,' the operator says curtly and types in the number. 'Thank you for using AT and T.' The bell is loud and shrill this time, as though I'm calling a person in the next room. Somebody answers on the fifth ring, but they don't say a word.

'Hello, Ruth?' I say. 'It's me, Freeman.'

Then this strangely familiar music fades in, a cross between game-show jazz and the music on a porno movie soundtrack, and I realize that I'm talking to an answering machine. 'You have reached a person who has been disconnected or is no longer in service,' a man's voice says – it's a young guy trying to sound like an announcer. 'Don't bother redialing. Ruth's in permanent space right now.' I can hear Ruth laughing in the background of the tape, that high squeal of a laugh she gets when she watches *Looney Tunes*. 'Ruth,' I say, 'it's me, Freeman.' But the tape clicks off before I can leave a message and then I get the dial tone.

I turn around feeling Maybelline's presence, but the hall's deserted. Just the long row of numbered doors and the ice machine. The room next to Maybelline's is open and I can see a TV going but I can't see the person who's watching it. At Christmas every year Ruth looks at *Going My Way* because her father has a tiny part in it. You can only see him for a second – he's one of the Choir Boys humming along when Bing says, 'Or would you rather be a pig?'

I turn and am headed back to my room when the pay phone rings.

'Hello, Ruth?' I say.

52

'Thirty-five cents please,' a woman with a kind voice says. 'Please deposit thirty-five cents.'

'OK,' I tell her, checking my pockets for change, and when the voice repeats itself using all the wrong inflections, I realize that I'm talking to another machine.

Vicki's got the cards out and she's dealing hands of poker, a game I was never very good at. It's just about dark now and the lighthouse is sweeping the desert, arcing out toward Liberty in the north and then panning east across the Wild Deuce before it fades out somewhere over the Great Basin. The lighthouse is one of these sucker attractions like The Trees of Mystery or Confusion Hill that Ruth and I used to stop at for grins, only it's been declared an official monument by the state of Nevada. This crazy German named Luther Kirschbaum migrated here at the turn of the century and convinced himself that the Big Rain was coming soon and would wash away everything west of where the town is now. So he built the lighthouse thinking that when the flood came Noah in his Ark would see the beacon and naturally just cruise by to save everyone. Vicki explains it much better in the tour, of course, with a whole lot of winking and too much emotion. She really plays it up big at the end, the part where Luther dies of thirst in his own lighthouse waiting for the rain that never fell. It helps to know that Luther was ninety-three years old at the time, but Vicki always manages to withhold that information.

'Freebee, honey,' Vicki says and throws a silver dollar in the kitty. 'You got to have a little faith. Hasn't everything worked out up to now?'

She reaches over to the Coleman lantern on the night stand and turns down the little key until the mantles glow a soft, breathing amber. She doesn't like the hotel lights because they make a person look old, she says, and God knows the desert does enough of that already.

I glance over at Vicki's cards – she's got them fanned behind her head like war feathers – and then check out her poker face, the tour-guide special. She makes me sit Indian-style when she deals Indian poker, which is nine out of every ten hands. The other games she deals aren't in Hoyle either, which usually means that half the deck is wild or that you don't know what your cards are until you turn them over. At least in this game I can see Vicki's hand (two pairs, queens and sevens), even if I can't see my own. I don't like what I see and, more importantly, I don't like what I can't see.

'I fold,' I say and set my cards face down on the bedspread. Vicki really does look better in this light. Her let-down hair has the consistency of spun sugar and her eyes seem to go deeper than their sockets. She claims she was a Miss Montana once and right now I have every reason to believe her.

'You had a little boat,' Vicki says gleefully and flips up my cards, what would have been the winning hand. 'Sixes over fives. Maybe you'll bet it next time.' She scoops up the kitty – eight pennies and her silver dollar – and lets it trickle into the folds of her dress with the rest of my change. 'You should know by now I always bluff.'

'I'm a slow learner,' I say.

'No you're not,' she says smiling, 'you're just slow to act.' She takes my hand and spreads it open, palm up, and runs her finger slowly along my lifeline. 'You have the same hands as Billy,' she says. 'When I first met him he was exactly like you, only he was staying at his mom's place on the reservation waiting for the draft board to call his number.' She picks up the bottle of Everclear that's wedged in one of her iguana-skin boots and takes a tiny little sip. 'We were doing shooters one night at the Mad River Rose and he told me he'd marry me if his number was three-sixty or above. Next morning he drew three-sixty on the nose. You should've seen his face. I swear he was thinking of enlisting.'

'He wound up marrying you. Isn't that what you wanted?'

She turns and looks absently into the mirror over my dresser, her bare, parched back exploding like a flash cube every time the lighthouse shines into my room. 'Bill called me last night from Reno,' she says. 'He can't make it till tomorrow. The highway's closed on account of black ice.'

I start to ask her what Bill's doing in Reno, especially since mercury claims are filed at the BLM office in Lovelock, but I can tell she doesn't know why he's there either. A lot of people pick up quick divorces in Reno, I know that much, though oddly enough that's where my folks got married. Vicki hasn't seen Bill since Halloween night, at a Grateful Dead show in Vegas. They got in a big fracas after Bill spent most of their money on some cocaine that turned out to be vitamin B-1. Vicki says Bill must have the healthiest nose in the state of Nevada by now.

'So you're stuck here with me,' I say. 'I guess that's the luck of the draw.'

'I would have picked here anyway,' she says and sits down on the bed next to me. She leans over and helps herself to a Chesterfield from the pack in my shirt pocket. 'What about you, Freeman?' she asks, crossing her noticeable legs. 'Is this where you want to be?'

Her face is so close to mine that I can't get a reading from it, and my first impulse is to laugh, though not out of confidence, the way Ruth always laughed and I always wanted to. I try not to think about the future until it's too late, so then it's not the future anymore, but I can't help thinking if Ruth doesn't show tonight the future will be like this forever.

'I guess you don't have to answer that right now,' Vicki says and backs away. She sticks her cigarette inside the lantern and lights it on one of the mantles. 'We've got a little time yet.'

She stands up and paces to the window, heel to toe, not once staggering but somehow swaying her hips, even though she's put away almost a full pint of Everclear. 'Bill and I used to practice this one when we got drunk,' she says. 'And that little finger exercise where you touch the end of your nose.' She demonstrates flawlessly. 'He never did get a 502, but he got picked up once for arson. It was about a month after we got here and I wanted him back – I

56

didn't have any friends in town and I figured I shouldn't have to be alone.'

She takes a long drag and blows it out the window. The smoke hangs just long enough for the lighthouse to paint it. 'Somebody had just torched the Laundromat in town, so I called up the sheriff – I didn't leave my name – and told him that Bill was his man. I said he was hiding out in the Stillwaters and that he was armed and dangerous, and then I described him right down to his last nose hair. They went after him the next day with hounds and they dragged him all the way down the mountain for questioning, and when they kicked him loose, he didn't even come to see me, just hauled himself up the mountain again with his stupid pickaxes. I had to buy a deputy five shots of Cuervo before he'd tell me what happened. Bill never once mentioned getting busted. The bastard wouldn't give me the satisfaction.'

She leans out the window, singing softly and a little off key and I swear for a second that it's not Vicki, that it's someone younger, softer, less rehearsed. 'Oh where have you been, Billy Boy, Billy Boy? Oh where have you been, charming Billy?' And then the light fills the room again and drains off and Vicki says in her normal voice, 'Fucking lighthouse. It makes it like a prison movie in here.'

This is the first time I've ever seen Vicki Whitehorse cry and it makes me want to cry myself, though not because I'm feeling sorry for *her*. I can't honestly say I want to be Vicki's lover and I can't say I don't want to either. Sometimes I think my heart's stuck on vacillation, like one of those crystals they put in all the new watches.

I gather up the cards on my bed and walk over to Vicki, careful to stay in the dark. 'Fifty-two card pickup,' I say and hurl the deck of cards out the window and we both watch as they fly out into the desert like the pages from a year-old calendar.

'I'd rather be good than lucky, anyway,' Vicki says. 'Billy Boy will be here in the morning. Someone's got to help him spend his fortune.'

'It might as well be you,' I say and shade my eyes from the lighthouse.

The neon sign on the Wild Deuce shows four cards to a heart flush plus the two of spades, which flashes on and off, I suppose, to indicate it's wild. They don't play poker with wild cards in the hotel casino, so if you drew the hand they show up on the sign, you'd have practically the worst cards you can get; a pair of treys would beat you.

I'm watching that sign recede in my rearview mirror as I head due west on Route 50 with all my worldly belongings. There are clouds overhead and I can't see the moon or the stars and it makes me think of the joke my father used to tell when all hope was lost, that the darkest hour is just before the storm. The radio's tuned to a station in Texas and they're playing that old Tom Jones song 'What's New, Pussycat?' and it's coming in as clear as if it was being broadcast back in Lighthouse. Vicki gave me a St Christopher medal before I left and I've got it around my neck, 'where all good surfers wear them,' she told me. I said I'd been waxing my board

58

for six months now, and she laughed out loud for quite a while after that, a happy laugh I don't remember her ever laughing, like the one I hope Ruth and I will share someday. It's hard to know what your choices are when everything's a choice, but at least you know momentum gives you one. And if Ruth Ann Chaney is headed in a different direction, then I'll just keep going in mine, right out into the desert with my high beams blazing, like old Luther Kirschbaum in his lighthouse.

I'm riding in the wake of a semi bearing Louisiana plates and tire flaps that have hula girls painted on them. There's nobody coming in the other direction, so I pull out in the left-hand lane, giving the driver the honk signal as I pass him, and he pulls off a long one that I hear slow down and finally fade away as I turn off down the dark dirt road toward the lighthouse. Bill has told me he's seen the beacon from Dancer's Ferry, which is up in the Stillwaters just outside of Cody, and sometimes late at night I wonder if maybe Ruth has seen it all the way in Phoenix, even if she couldn't tell it from a shooting star.

I roll down the windows and let the air fill up the camper until I feel like I don't have any weight. All-Nite Ray, the deejay, gives the weather for El Paso, and I know it's going to rain before the first drop hits my windshield.

WE FIND OURSELVES IN
MOONTOWN

Keepnews didn't want the sailor to get any ideas so he set his coolie hat on the chair beside him and his satchel on the chair beside that. It was bad enough that they didn't have onions for your chilidog, but then they let riffraff like Sailorboy sit at the counter and make eyes at you while you tried to fetch a napkin.

I can get all the riffraff I want back home, Keepnews told himself. If they have riffraff everywhere, why can't they have onions?

The page was mispronouncing his name over the PA for the umpteenth time. He unfolded the paper napkin and carefully draped it over his silk pants, laying the chilidog across his legs. Then he leaned back in his chair and closed his eyes. He had chosen this corner of the airport lobby deliberately, away from the tourists and the slot machines that played parts of 'Ta-ra-ra-boom-dee-ay' if you won, and the hawkers who had tried to sell him a fake leather flight bag as the real McCoy. But there was always something to remove you from your peace once you'd found it, Keepnews decided, and in this case he was certain it was his mother whom he'd promised to call when he arrived safely in Reno but never had. It was his mother who had talked him into taking the Fun Train up from Oakland in the first place and, as Keepnews figured it, it was his mother who could share his miserable weekend: the motion sickness on the train, the dim little room with the red felt wallpaper and the spastic TV, the two hours of blackjack that had left him nearly broke.

Keepnews turned and glanced quickly past Sailorboy to the clock in the snack bar. His plane would be leaving in another half hour. 'The Fun Train can just go back without me,' he mumbled.

When he swiveled around again to eat his chilidog, there were three ladies standing in front of him, all with the same look of shameless curiosity on their faces. 'You always talk to yourself?' the woman in the middle asked. She vaguely resembled his mother: sixtyish, tall, with a body people politely called 'big-boned'. She was darker than his mother, though, a distinction Keepnews hoped meant greater differences. The other women were much smaller and were carrying gift-boxed gambling sets: cards, dice, miniature roulette wheels. Keepnews could imagine them playing poker with their grandchildren, taking them for what little they had, and compensating them with hollow chocolate bunnies at Easter.

'I'm my own best company,' Keepnews said and grinned broadly, though he was glaring at the women through his sunglasses. 'That's why I always get in the last word.'

'No one ever got in the last word on Cel,' one of the small ladies said and laughed. The woman who looked like Keepnews's mother smiled in a fashion that revealed a long-standing animosity toward her friend. 'Morgan Keepnews, Morgan Keepnews, to the white courtesy phone, please,' the page said again, with the accent squarely on the *news*.

There was a pause and Keepnews wondered if he had flinched at the sound of his own mispronounced name. Then one of the small ladies got antsy. 'Cel wanted to ask you a question,' she said and this time the large woman's face flushed with so much animosity that there was no room left for the smile.

'We thought you was a movie star,' the large woman said quickly. 'I told Megan I seen you on *The Edge of Night*. You played a police detective, didn't you?' She turned to the lady who had so far been mute. 'They found out he was making snuff movies on the side, and when they tried to arrest him, he drove his car into the river.'

'On purpose?' the small lady asked, and the large woman looked disgustedly down the long airport corridor, where some men were having their pointy-toed boots shined.

'I've only been on the TV once,' Keepnews said, 'and that was on nighttime *Jeopardy*.' Really, he had never appeared on television, but he thought that a small, well-timed lie might free him sooner than the truth. In Keepnews's opinion the one advantage of travel was the fact that nobody knew who you were.

'I watch *Jeopardy* every night,' the large woman said. 'I don't recall seeing any black folks on there.'

'I must look thinner in person,' Keepnews said. 'My mother always told me the camera puts on twenty pounds, but I never believed her until now. I guess it doesn't pay to disbelieve your mother.'

The small ladies started to giggle, which only served to make the large woman's interrogation more hostile. She glared ferociously at Keepnews. 'You call yourself black, don't you?'

'Yes, ma'am,' Keepnews said and smiled. 'But I'm the whitest nigger I know.'

'Is that right?' the large woman said and pushed up her glasses on her nose. The small women seemed to take this as a sign that they shouldn't laugh, though Keepnews could see that they still thought something was funny. 'You have a name?' the large woman asked him.

He considered lying, and then remembered that this strategy had backfired on him the last time. You had certain privileges when you were black, he thought, just as you did when you were white. The trouble was they were privileges nobody wanted, like the company of strange women in airports who would talk to you solely because you were of the same race. 'Keepnews,' he said finally, imitating the page. 'Morgan Keepnews.'

'Sounds like a bird,' one of the small ladies said.

The large woman broke in excitedly: 'I've heard that name before. Where you from, Mr Keepnews?'

'Oakland, California,' Keepnews said and sat forward. 'Now what kind of movie star lives in Oakland, California?'

'Reggie,' one of the small ladies said.

'So you never been on *The Edge of Night*, is that what you're telling me?' The large woman folded her arms across her massive bosom.

'Yes, ma'am,' Keepnews said.

'I thought for sure you was in showbiz,' she said. 'The way you was dressed and all. How come you're wearing those belly-dancer pants then?' She turned to her friends who were freely laughing now. 'Maybe we should call him Morganna.'

Keepnews took off his sunglasses so that they could see he was done humoring them. You could wear anything you wanted to in Gambletown, he wanted to say. That was all part of it, to show you had nothing to lose. It would be a different story back home, of course. The dropouts at the security company where he worked would call him Queen-for-a-day. They would ride him in the locker room in the morning when he changed into his uniform and they would call him at Shack 9 on his walky-talky, 'Queen-for-a-day, over, talk dirty to me, over.' And at quitting time they would whistle at him and make catcalls and he would shake it for them when he walked out the door, bowing to pick up the rolled-up dollar bills they had thrown, like a stripper at the Borderline Saloon.

'But this is Gambletown,' Keepnews said under his breath, and he picked up his coolie hat, a gift his brother, Jerome, had sent him from Saigon near the end of the war, and positioned it on his balding head. Keepnews had been excused from the draft because of his asthma.

'*Combien pour ta soeur?*' he asked the ladies and just as he said it a slot machine started playing 'Ta-ra-ra-boom-dee-ay' and played it all the way through to the end. The man who had pulled the handle started whooping and hugging the woman standing next to him, and then he leaned down and kissed the face of the slot machine for a long time.

The ladies abandoned Keepnews all at once, scurrying over to the winner, who was now rolling around on the floor. Keepnews watched them until they had been surrounded by other onlookers and he could just see the top of the large woman's wig. He looked away, in the direction of the clock, but his gaze fell instead on Sailorboy, who was leaning on a pillar in the foreground watching the hoopla. Sailorboy turned his head and flashed Keepnews an infantile grin. Keepnews picked up his chilidog and took a large bite. It was cold.

'*Laquelle*,' Sailorboy said, approaching Keepnews, '*la grosse ou la malade?*'

Keepnews looked up at Sailorboy's peaked face: his crewcut made his head look too small for his body, and his body looked too small for an adult's. If it wasn't for the uniform, Keepnews was sure he'd take this white boy for a retard.

'*La grosse ou la malade?*' Sailorboy repeated.

Keepnews took another bite of chilidog. He didn't know how to speak French except for that one phrase his brother had taught him, and he wasn't even sure what it meant, besides that it was an insult. 'Ain't you a long ways from the ocean?' he said, deliberately skewing his grammar.

'Depends on what you call the ocean,' Sailorboy said. 'The moon's got oceans only they don't have no water.'

Keepnews started to laugh and then consciously stopped himself. 'You're a longer ways from the moon,' he said.

66

'Depends on what you call the moon,' Sailorboy said and sat down in the chair vacated by Keepnews's hat. They stared out the tinted-glass wall at the runway, which seemed to originate at the base of the Sierras. A DC-9 with a large, symmetrical smile painted on its face was taxiing toward them. Keepnews decided it looked like Sailorboy.

'You from around here?' Sailorboy asked, still staring out the window.

'Sometimes,' Keepnews said. The cheese had congealed on his chilidog and he was tweezing it off with his fingers.

'Man,' Sailorboy said and wiped his face with his hand. 'You got to say the words in the Navy. If you don't say the words they send you to Happy Hour. Happy Hour ain't so happy in the Navy.' Sailorboy moved his face so close to Keepnews's that he could feel and smell his breath. 'You just say the words, man, and I'll split. Go ahead, say them.'

Keepnews took the bandage of cheese and carefully laid it in the cylindrical ashtray by his side. 'My mama told me never to talk to strangers,' he said. 'If you was to ask me, I'd say you was pretty strange.'

Sailorboy stared at Keepnews for several seconds and then leaned back in his chair, smiling. 'I've got family myself,' he said at last. 'Got a sister in New Orleans and a stepsister in Miami. The rest bought it one way or another.' He sat back in his chair again and perched his sailor hat in his lap. '*I* almost bought it awhile back. Tried to asphyxiate myself, in a two-car garage in Shreveport. The gauge said there was half a tank, but in ten minutes the Dodge was out of gas.' Sailorboy was shaking his head.

'My sister said it was a sign from God. She said He spared me 'cause I look like Jesus. I told her Jesus was a hippie.' He turned and faced Keepnews again. 'I ain't no hippie,' Sailorboy said.

'State your business,' Keepnews said. 'I don't like news until six o'clock.'

Sailorboy fidgeted and then took out a large turquoise-and-silver necklace from his peacoat and draped it over his knee. 'I stole this one from my stepsister. Would've stole it from my sister if it had been hers.'

'I hope you don't expect me to buy that from you,' Keepnews said. A woman in a purple uniform announced that Flight 606 to Oakland was now boarding. 'If I wore that I'd have to learn the raindance.'

'Thought I'd trade it,' Sailorboy said.

'Oh yeah?' Keepnews said and Sailorboy looked at him the way he had at the snack bar, the way his brother had looked when he was on heroin, like just touching him would make him explode. 'What do you think I got in my bag?' Keepnews said, disbelieving. 'I ain't no doctor.'

'Nobody said you was,' Sailorboy said and looked off toward the mountains again.

'This is tombstone country, man,' Keepnews said and Sailorboy's face lit up as though he were a small child, as though he would believe anything Keepnews told him. Keepnews wondered what his mother would think about that; she *dis*believed everything he told her, even on the morning he called her from the police station to tell her that Jerome had passed away.

'Death Valley,' Keepnews said. 'We find ourselves in Moontown.'

'I heard that,' Sailorboy said.

The lobby emptied out except for Keepnews and
Sailorboy and then the woman in the purple uniform
made her final announcement: 'Last call for PSA
Flight 606 servicing Oakland.' Keepnews decided
that he didn't want to go home just yet, that his
mother deserved a little more suspense. He had
only met his brother's dealer once, but he was sure
he could play him convincingly enough.

'You willing to travel?' Keepnews said. 'I can't be
conducting my business in airports.'

Sailorboy nodded.

'Well, I hope you got some transportation then,'
Keepnews said and began fanning himself with his
coolie hat.

Sailorboy fished some keys out of his trousers
and set them on his leg next to the Indian necklace.
He had a wide, conspiratorial grin on his face. 'I
was hoping you'd pull me in your rickshaw,' he
said.

At Keepnews's suggestion, they pulled into the
drive-thru at Wendy's first thing. Sailorboy said he
wouldn't eat no square hamburger, so he ordered
three frosties and a large fries and told the girl
through the speaker that he liked the sound of her
voice. Keepnews ordered a chilidog, with extra
onions and no cheese. The sun had practically
set now and it was getting cold and someone
had carved a hole in the plastic rear window of
Sailorboy's convertible. Keepnews shivered and

stared out the wind wing, at the casinos on the next street over. The series lights were just beginning their cycles, and above them vapor trails from an invisible jet could still be seen against the dark pink sky.

'You have a heater in this thing?' Keepnews asked.

'Broken,' Sailorboy said and spooned a large bite of ice cream into his mouth.

'You ain't dumb enough to steal a car with no heater, are you?'

'Registration's in the glove box,' Sailorboy said. 'I never had the occasion to steal an automobile. Stole the tires off a dune buggy once. Floated down the Rio Grande on the inner tubes, all the way to Albuquerque.'

Keepnews switched on the radio. A preacher was telling a female caller that she should strip before God. Keepnews switched it off again. 'Turn left at this next light,' he told Sailorboy. He didn't have any idea where he was going.

They kept driving away from the Strip with Keepnews giving directions. He told Sailorboy that you could never be too careful, that there were G-men everywhere watching your every move and that they hated you more if you were innocent. Sailorboy kept looking in the rearview mirror after that, and when they turned into a residential neighborhood, he narrowly missed hitting a small child on some Big Wheels. The car fishtailed in a cul-de-sac and wound up with its back end on the sidewalk.

'Sloppy,' Keepnews said. His sunglasses had

70

flown off his face and he was rummaging for them in the crevice between his seat and the gearbox.

Sailorboy shut off the engine and the car shuddered before dying. 'I walled,' he said and looked in the rearview mirror. He could see the bright light of a television glowing in the darkened house behind them.

'You what?' Keepnews said.

'A-W-O-L,' Sailorboy said. 'A Woman Of Leisure. That's what they call you if you split.' He looked up into the cottonwood trees that surrounded them and then laid his head on the red plastic dashboard. His face had taken on a new blankness. 'The owls are watching us too, man,' he said.

'I'm the only one watching you,' Keepnews said angrily. 'You just do like you're told and you'll be fine.' It was guys like Sailorboy who made you never want to leave your room, who were always fucking up and making you feel it so they wouldn't have to. The rest of the world was guys like your mother. Guys who wouldn't let you feel a thing.

'We're going to the highway now,' Keepnews said, regaining his composure. He looked down and noticed that the fleshy part of his hand, between his thumb and index finger, was bleeding. He had jammed it on the glove-box door when Sailorboy had lost control of the car. He pulled his cuff down over the wound and closed his fist around it. 'We have to circumvent our circumvention,' he told Sailorboy. 'That's how you get to where you're going.' He shut his eyes and tried not to think about the pain. 'You should've told me you were hot,' he said.

Sailorboy started the engine again. 'You wouldn't have dealed,' he said and pulled the car off the sidewalk and out onto the unlit street.

Sailorboy kept his eyes on the road the whole time and Keepnews didn't look back either. The highway was deserted except for a few trucks going the other way, toward Reno, so Sailorboy was flooring it, the car lifting off the ground after each swell in the road. Keepnews's hand was throbbing and some blood had seeped through his cuff onto his silk pants. He covered up the stain with the Wendy's bag and looked benignly out the window. There was no moon and he couldn't see the features of the land, just the black depth he was sure must stretch on for miles. It was like what they said about the universe, that there was nothing in your life for years at a time and then, boom, you came up on this new shit and it overwhelmed you, and you couldn't remember what happened in your life before. There was no preparing for that new shit either, just a long time to fret about it in between.

Sailorboy exited the highway without being told, though it was exactly what Keepnews had intended him to do. It suddenly occurred to Keepnews that he couldn't see the moon because this *was* the moon, just like he'd said, and that they were driving around in the Land-Rover looking for a place to put up the flag. He started to laugh.

Sailorboy looked at him with frightened eyes. 'What's so funny?'

'I speak the truth,' Keepnews said, 'even when I don't want to.' He threw back his head and laughed

72

loudly, falsely, and then he remembered a nonsense joke his brother had told him when they were still in high school. It was a joke designed to expose people as fakes, to see if they would laugh at a punch line that wasn't funny. 'How many pancakes does it take to get to the moon?' Keepnews asked Sailorboy. 'How many fucking buttermilk pancakes does it take, man?'

Sailorboy ran his hand along his jaw and looked straight ahead.

'Three rats and a motorcycle,' Keepnews blurted out, but Sailorboy didn't laugh. The car was slowing gradually to a halt even though Sailorboy was still pressing down on the gas pedal. The gauge said there was half a tank. Amazed, they both watched the broken white line in front of them until it wasn't moving anymore.

Sailorboy turned off the headlights and they sat there in the car in the middle of the road without saying anything. There was no traffic, no crickets, no wind, no moon, no sound except the sound they made themselves. Sailorboy moved his hand onto Keepnews's hand, the good one, and began rubbing it softly between the fingers. Keepnews was thinking about his mother back on earth, alone in the parlor where she stayed up nights when she couldn't sleep, reading her Bible line by line, smiling when Jesus smiled, weeping when Jesus wept. And he was thinking about his brother, Jerome, and the turn his soul had taken and the new shit he must be dealing with now, and how it made him forget about his life back on earth. And he was thinking how *he* could remember everything, the house where he lived, the color of its paint, the names of the people who lived there.

He wanted to confess. He wanted to tell Sailorboy everything. He brought his wounded hand up to his face. It wasn't bleeding anymore. He gently picked up Sailorboy's hand and just as gently placed it at Sailorboy's side.

'I'm a virgin,' Keepnews said proudly, and Sailorboy, with equal aplomb, declared, 'So am I.'

FRED'S LID

Really what I want to do is record my solo album for a while and then when I'm done – I never finish that sentence because I can never think what comes next. They have everything covered in English where this comma goes after this coordinating conjunction or why that's a dependent clause with an adverb modifier, etc., but they never tell you what to do when you run out of things to say. Fragment, they tell you. Just to make you feel bad. As if you don't feel bad enough already. I'm thinking all this while I lie on my front lawn with the recorder going, capturing this brilliant rendition of the sky (so far there's a whole lot of sky on my solo album), when out of nowhere Me drives up in Shirley's Buick Electra. Me's short for Mia, who is Fred's recurrent girl friend. Shirley's Me's mom.

'Nice wheels,' I say. The Electra looks a lot different when Me's driving it, maybe because she's so small. Shirley's in Maui right now with this new guy, Rick.

'Shirley forgot to take the keys,' Me says. She looks sad, but you can tell it's not about what she just said. Everybody likes wheels. 'Fred's old man,' she says and tilts her head toward the dashboard. 'He found Fred's lid.'

When she tells me this I don't picture anything, except the mileage on the Electra, which I'm staring at already. 064001. Once I was in the parking lot at Safeway waiting for my mom and I swear the odometer on the wagon turned over by itself. 'You mean Fred's busted?' I say.

She nods and looks at me in her serious manner, like Joe Friday on *Dragnet* when he informs the next of kin. 'His old man says he's going to have him arrested, but before that he's grounded indefinitely.' I stare at Me while Me stares out the windshield. Her skin is almost pink, like one of those fragile salamanders that evolve in caves, and for a second I understand why Me and Fred always take each other back.

'Can you believe it?' she says.

'No,' I say.

She pushes the button that raises all the windows and her face gets this pained look, like she's doing something really strenuous. A few strands of her hair get caught in the window, but she doesn't do anything about it, just puts the Electra in low and drifts away.

I go into the house and get the masking tape and the little film can where I keep my dope. I figure we're effectively dead from this moment on, because if Fred's busted we're all busted, especially since Fred taught us what little we know. I haven't told anyone about the seventy-five hours of detention that I have to serve before I can graduate, which technically is impossible with only ten days left of school.

I roll a little stinger out of the last of my dope on a copy of *House Beautiful* and go back outside. I can pretty much remember the shape of my body, because there's an indentation in the lawn where I was lying, but the masking tape doesn't stick very well to grass. On *Dragnet* they always happen to find the bodies on asphalt.

En route to tell Monkey Boy, I rewind the tape to see if you can hear the news. It was Fred who convinced me to work on my solo album because, as he put it, what else *could* I work on after the Beatles gave each other their walking papers? He said it didn't matter that I couldn't play an instrument, just as long as I got my DNA down on tape. Fred has lots to say about the new science. He wants to be an entomologist.

I hang back a little when I get near Monkey Boy's house, to see if there's any authority figures around. On the tape, what you can hear is in this order: sky, the Electra, people talking minus the words. This could be what DNA sounds like. Monkey Boy has a pulley rigged up in the eucalyptus tree over the garage and he's hauling up a chair from the dinette furniture that his mom left out for Goodwill. It's Senior Ditch Day today, which really means you get to be with the people you're trying to get away from when you ditch, except that it's at the location of *their* choice (I cut the day they voted), which *really* means one of the five spots Mr Grossbeak, our principal, picked for them. And naturally they chose the beach club in Malibu with the sauna and the volleyball courts and the swimming pool, even though the place is right next to the ocean. They think it's a sneak preview for the rest of their lives.

As for us, we shined it all on so we could vous over at Me's, but I guess that's off now that Fred's doing time. Fred's old man says we never get beamed down on the right planet, even when we're at the controls.

When I get to the driveway, Monkey Boy is walking out of the house with his mom's portable TV and a big yellow extension cord. He's reeking of dope. 'Let's *Dragnet*,' he says. I can't see his eyes through his wraparounds, so it's hard to know if he said it to me or if he was just saying it anyway. He plugs in the TV on the side of the house and we climb up the eucalyptus to the top of the garage.

'UA,' Monkey Boy says, smiling and shaking his head as though he's just now noticed I'm here. That's what everyone calls me, UA, except for my folks, who still call me Robert. In Algebra I used a pair of dice once to answer a multiple-choice test and Mr Kramer, my teacher, got mad even though we were studying probabilities. He sent a letter to my mom that said, with a lot of other stuff, that I was an underachiever. I got a C on the test. I'm pretty sure that's what *really* ticked Mr Kramer off.

'Did you hear about Fred?' I ask Monkey Boy.

He looks in my direction but doesn't say anything. It's near the end of *Dragnet*, the part where the announcer reads the crooks' sentences while the crooks try to look innocent and remorseful all at the same time. It seems like a tough part, but I'm con-

78

vinced Monkey Boy could play it – he always looks
that way.

'I like it up here,' Monkey Boy says. 'I think everybody should live outside and have their backyards
inside. You know, like a big terrarium.' He takes off
his shades and looks at me. 'I don't even want to
know what that masking tape's for.' He laughs until
you can tell he can't remember why. 'Can you
believe this jive about Fred?' he says. 'His old man
told me he's going to join the Air Force. That's
spooky weird if you ask me. Go ahead ask me.'

That's what Monkey Boy always says when he
calls something spooky weird. He doesn't really
expect you to ask him. I start to laugh and stop and
then Monkey Boy laughs and then I laugh with him.
On the TV, *Ozzie and Harriet* is just coming on. It's
one of the in-between episodes, before Rick's
married but after he's the Irrepressible Ricky. My
favorites are when Ricky does one of those old rock
'n' roll numbers that some black guy did originally,
but never got credit for, at least not by the people
who watch *Ozzie and Harriet*. I like it when they
pan the audience and there're these actors who are
supposed to be teenagers but they look a lot older
and they're in suits and ties kind of smiling and
nodding to the music but without really moving the
rest of their bodies. You can tell they have a lot
going for them because nobody would like them if
they didn't, and they always have plenty of buddies.
These are the kind of guys with futures, I think.
Then I think it's too bad they're all old guys by now.

I make a crack about Ricky's haircut, but Monkey
Boy's not watching the TV anymore. He's into the

79

slow part of the dope, the part where all these shows we watch seem like they really mean something. His face is changing every five seconds or so. Right now he's smiling. Now he's staring. Now he looks pretty sad. I start to ask him if he really heard Fred was joining the Air Force but it comes out 'What are we going to do?' This is probably only the second or third time I've asked him a direct question in the year that I've known him.

After a while he says, 'I've got an idea,' and his face gets bright again.

I wait a long time, but he never tells me what it is.

The next day at school, Fred's not in PE, which is no big deal since he really hates swimming (according to Fred, Coach Marty's a closet and he just likes to see us in our bunhuggers), but when he doesn't show up for Am. Gov., I get depressed. Fred always shows up for Am. Gov. I'm so depressed that I have to cut Driver's Ed. and Photography and walk the three miles home. I smoke my last bit of roach under the house and then sit in my parents' bedroom by the phone thinking that Fred will probably call. The phone rings. It's my mom.

'Robert,' she says, 'do you remember what day it is?'

It's hard for me to forget since she left me notes on the stove island and the refrigerator and the door inside my closet. I can tell by her voice that she still hasn't heard about Fred.

'It's picture day,' I say.

'And what time's your appointment?'

'Four-thirty.'

'Well, don't you think you better get going?'

'I guess so,' I say. I can hear other people talking on the phone, but their voices are way in the distance and I wonder if they can hear us. I try to imagine what my voice must sound like. It must sound pretty strange, I decide. 'Robert,' my mom says and laughs, 'what haven't you been doing in school today?'

I don't know what to say to this. So I don't say anything. I can hear a woman in the background. She sounds like she's in the shower, singing.

'Robert,' my mom says again, 'I was only kidding.'

'I know.'

'I'll see you tonight,' she says. 'Don't forget to comb your hair. Bye bye.'

I put some Murine in my eyes to take out the red from the dope (one of Fred's major rules) and ride my bike downtown to the photographer's. I missed the day at school when they took graduation pictures. Last year I was absent too and my name fell under the category 'Camera Shy' in the back of the year-book. 'Camera Shy' winds up being a list of the prominent truants at our high school. Fred says that Grossbeak uses it when he decides which parents to call into his office. So far I've been spared.

When I come in the door, Mr Hansen, the photographer, doesn't look up, even though a little buzzer goes off. He's frowning as he x's out pictures on one of those elementary-school sheets, one out of a big stack on his desk. None of the kids look very happy. It must be a hard job trying to make people smile all the time.

'I'm here to get my picture taken,' I say.

'What's your name?'

'Robert,' I say. 'Robert Parks.'

'Oh, right,' he says. 'You're the graduation.' He looks at me and tries to smile, but I don't think he recognizes me. He's the father of a friend of mine, or an ex-friend of mine – Troy pretty much split with us when we started smoking dope. He really believed all those drug movies they showed us in Jay-Are High, the kind where the good kid gets pressured into smoking dope by the bad kids and then sees himself in the mirror and his face looks like Play-Doh. Those movies used to scare me too, but I guess I forgot about them, along with everything else I learned there. Troy was always a better student than I was.

We go into a little room that's empty except for Mr Hansen's equipment and a white blanket that's thumb-tacked to the wall. Mr Hansen gives me this costume to put over my clothes. It's a combination shirt-and-tie graduation gown, only the thing cuts off around the shoulders. I think about asking Mr Hansen if he'll take a picture of my whole body instead of just my head, but he looks so tired and sad standing behind the camera that I just do everything he says, even smile. I take a lot of pictures of myself in the little booth down at Thriftymart, but they always come out the same. I found a picture from when I was in Cub Scouts, in the junk drawer underneath the hole punch and a pin cushion in the shape of a tomato. Everyone else in the picture has these creased smiles, but I'm standing at the end looking past the camera at something that's making me wince. I plan on using all the pictures on the inside jacket of my solo album. The caption's going to say: 'Before and Before.'

When I get outside, the light from Mr Hansen's flash makes everything look cut in half. I lean on my bike, focusing on the car that's parked right in front of me. It's Shirley's Electra. For a second I lose track of where I am.

'UA,' Troy says from the passenger seat, 'we've got to stop meeting like this.'

'I guess so,' I say. Troy always did have a lame sense of humor. He's one of the few people I resent calling me UA. I lean down and see Mia sitting on the other side of him, trying to look like nothing's weird. Troy was always such a squirrelly little guy and then one day every girl I know started saying he was cute.

'Did my father say cheese,' Troy says, 'or did he promise you a lollipop?'

'He did cartwheels,' I say. I turn and pick up my bike, feeling grateful that it's downhill for the next few blocks. It's times like these when I wonder if there's a career in sadness, if somebody would pay me to just sit behind a desk somewhere and think sad stuff all day long. I look over at Troy and as usual he's smiling perfectly, and I think about how we used to steal pens in third grade and never got caught for it, even when the teacher accused him directly. Mia's little hand turns the key in the ignition and then her little hand puts the car in drive. This is what the mileage says: 064010.

'I guess you heard about Fred,' Troy says and shakes his head in a too-bad kind of way. 'The hippie finds Jesus. Do you think he'll go to divinity school?' His laughter blends into rush hour as the car pulls away from the curb. The Electra just seems to get smaller and smaller instead of getting farther away.

At home, I smell a pie baking and I remember that it's bridge night and that it must be my mom's turn. As usual she's running around trying to straighten up things before the other moms arrive, which always puts her in a bad mood. I can never figure out how she sounds so nice when she opens the door for Mrs Brenner, who always comes early. Mrs Brenner really depresses me.

My mom tries to vacuum around me, moving the long hose underneath my legs while I sit on the couch, but she gets fed up pretty quick and kicks me out of the living room. Upstairs, my father's drinking a scotch and swearing at the news on TV. Scotch and bridge. That's what parents do.

'Robert,' my father says when he finally sees me, 'have a seat.'

It makes me nervous when my father is overly polite. It's the same tone my counselor gets when he asks me what trade school I plan on attending – he just assumes that I won't be going to college. I sink down in the beanbag chair (it's really filled with Styrofoam BBs) and wait for my father to say something. The anchorman is looking concerned about a fire in the valley. You can tell he doesn't really care.

'So do you have any plans?' my father says and sits forward. 'I mean for when you graduate.'

I'm going to finish my solo album, I want to say. But instead I say, 'I don't have any plans,' because I know this will make my father feel better.

'I got a call from Mr Grossbeak today,' my father says. He turns and looks at me now while at the

84

same time pressing the MUTE button on the TV controller. I can see him in my peripheral vision. 'He said if you take a class in summer school, you can make up the detention and graduate. Any class, he said.' He waits for me to say something. When I don't he gets up to adjust the antennae on the TV. Rabbit ears, he calls them. 'Robert,' he says, 'is there anything wrong?'

I shake my head No. Reality sucks is what I'm thinking. Fred tried to have that put on a T-shirt once but the lady wouldn't do it. She said he was too young.

'Adults are just big kids with lots of money,' my father says. 'Really,' he says as if I don't believe him. 'You just work your way up, that's all. How about a JC in the fall? I'm sure you can still get in.'

I know this conversation is designed to make me feel better, but it only makes me feel worse. 'All right,' I say and look at my feet. They look the same as they always do. My father sits on the couch again and we watch TV in silence, exiles from the world downstairs. Around ten, my mom comes up with two pieces of pie à la mode. She's in her fancy clothes and she's smoking a cigarette, something she never does except on bridge night. She says she doesn't inhale.

'How is everybody?' she says, looking directly at me.

'Fine,' I say.

'Good,' she says. 'I guess your father had a little talk with you.' She looks at my father, who nods. 'Good,' she says again. While we eat our pie, she tells us about what Mrs Brenner's kid plans on doing for the next twenty years. It makes me sad thinking about how different this is from the version that Mrs Brenner's kid must tell. But I try to look happy anyway just so my mom won't ask me any more questions. She takes our plates and goes downstairs. I can hear her say something that makes everybody laugh. The bridge ladies think my mom's a *scream*.

In another half hour my father's asleep on the couch and I sneak outside through the garage. The air feels good on my face as I ride my bike. I like the hissing noise it makes when you go down hills. Like cicadas. At Fred's, there's a note pinned on the front door:

To whom it may concern:

Fred is unavailable for the remainder of his adolescence.

Sincerely,
Fred's Old Man

PS This will be a very long time.

I go around back and crouch underneath Fred's window. He's sitting on the floor in his jammies, reading a book with this severe look on his face. The title is *Understanding Your Teenage Boy*. There's a Bible on the floor right next to him with a sock stuck in it for a bookmark.

He looks up just as I'm about to tap on the window. 'UA,' he mouths, as though he's been expecting me. He gets up to let me in. It takes me a while to figure out what's so different about him. Then it hits me. I've never seen Fred in his jammies before.

'What's the news?' Fred whispers. 'I haven't been able to call anyone. My old man has the phone locked up in his filing cabinet.'

'You,' I say. It feels so good to see Fred that I start to laugh.

'Oh yeah?' Fred says, 'What did you hear?'

'That your old man found your lid, that he's going to have you put in jail.'

'He already has me in jail.' He waves his hand across his body like a model on a game show. 'The lid was in my *Coleoptera* cigar box.' He grins. 'No beetles, just dope. I guess he got suspicious after Grossbeak called him.' He gives me an oh-well shrug of his shoulders. 'Who told you, anyway?'

'Mia,' I say and watch his face. He stares over at the window screen that's leaning on the sill. He looks kind of seasick.

'Me and Me are history,' he says finally. He pulls open a dresser drawer and brings out one of his bug containers, only it's got a picture of Mia in the place where a moth is supposed to go. 'Did you know that if you put caterpillars on the edge of a jar they'll follow each other forever?'

'Don't they turn into butterflies?'

'Yeah,' he says, 'they just never get wings.'

He picks up the Bible by his foot. 'Ever read this?' he asks me. I look at him and he looks serious. Then he smiles. 'Neither have I,' he says. 'It's pretty weird stuff. I don't know if I'll make it to the end.'

He rummages in the dresser and brings out a bottle that has FORMALDEHYDE written across it on a piece of masking tape. He takes a huge swallow. 'The eahdult pain reliever,' he says in a voice like an announcer's. 'My old man didn't get my *whole* stash.'

He offers me the bottle and I take a slug. I'm pretty sure it's gin. 'What are you going to do now?' I ask him and I realize that I sound like my father.

He gets this hazy look and then he lies down with his head propped up against his bed. 'I always wanted to be a deejay in the Third World,' he says. 'You know, play Lady Soul to all those Hindus while they kneel to their sacred cows.' He looks at me and I can tell that he's excited. 'It wouldn't be like food or anything,' he says, 'but it might make them feel better. There *has* to be a Radio Free India.'

I picture Fred in one of those broadcasting schools that they advertise during reruns and it makes me smile. 'Come down to Thriftymart with me,' I tell him. 'We'll get our picture taken together.'

'I wish,' he says, 'but my old man's been doing a lot of spot checks.' He reaches out and shakes my hand – another first – and I help him to his feet.

'You still hate life, don't you?' I ask him when I'm halfway out the window.

'Now more than ever,' he says and laughs.

The Thriftymart's in a field all by itself and from the freeway it looks like a big UFO, only square. I have a thing for the women who work the counter at the luncheonette. They always recognize me and say 'Hi,' but when they take my order they ask, 'What can I get for you, today?' as though I don't always order a jamocha shake. You never see people with bouffant hair except in Thriftymart. I want to know where they live.

I stand on the pad in front of the electric door for a long time before I go in. I'm thinking about India and Aretha Franklin and women with little dots on their foreheads, twisting like there's no tomorrow. And I'm thinking about Fred and how things change, but without you knowing what they've changed to. And I'm not thinking about anything, really. I'm really just alive.

I wave into the camera over aisle nine, and head past the Jell-O and the nail polish and the stuff you never think about until you run out of it. The photo booth is empty like always and I slip inside, shutting the little curtain behind me. I try to look neutral, but when the camera goes off I'm smiling baby-wide.

When I come back out, there's a man standing by a display of razors. He's about my father's age and build and there's a girl standing next to him who seems to be his daughter. She's cute, but a little young.

'Cat food,' the man says, 'what aisle?'

'Really?' I say. 'Do you really think I work here?' I look down at my hand, the hand that's holding the pictures. 'Does this look like me?' I ask him, but he's already looking for the cat-food aisle.

His daughter pipes in though. 'They don't do you justice,' she says looking at my pictures, and it's like she's been waiting her whole life to say it to me. 'They don't do you justice at all.'

PINOCCHIO'S

They had heard rush hour come and go while they waited for her boy friend, Frank, and now as if to fill the void, someone was practicing a harp in the flat upstairs. Richard thought the tune was 'Over the Rainbow', but he couldn't be sure because the harp kept starting and stopping in a new place, and Claire was vaguely humming along while she fooled with her eyes in the mirror. He stood at the open window behind her fanning himself with one of Frank's *Playboys*, a can of beer wedged between his neck and shoulder as if it were a telephone. He half expected to see Frank out there with the girl, telling her in a husky voice his joke about the three-balled tomcat. But there was no one, only the faded brick back of the Italian restaurant where someone had spray-painted REINVENT THE WORLD, and above this on the roof, a neon sign in the figure of Pinocchio with his nose growing long, then short, then long again. Richard decided that the nose might as well stay long; if Pinocchio wasn't lying then somebody else was.

'I don't look dumber than I look, do I?' Claire said into the mirror. She stubbed out her cigarette in an

91

ashtray on the TV, which had the sound turned down. 'I tell Frank I'm thinking about finishing my degree in Lib. Sci., and he tells me I'm dumber than I look. What a potatohead.'

She waited for Richard to say something, and when he didn't, she snuck up behind him. 'How's the sunset?' she whispered, running her finger up his neck to the earlobe. Richard startled and the can of beer fell to the carpet, where it rolled against some boxes of Frank and Claire's things that were stacked in a little pyramid by the radiator. She and Frank had been living in this place for two weeks now and they still hadn't put away their belongings. 'There goes your High Life,' Claire said matter-of-factly. 'I don't know why you can't just drink it.'

Richard turned and regarded her. She had only finished making up one side of her face, and he couldn't decide which half looked better. He had told her once that he respected her because she didn't wear makeup, but he found out later that she'd been wearing it that night and always had. 'Beer's a good conductor,' he said finally. 'That is, if you'd keep it in the refrigerator.'

She laughed. 'Woe is you,' she said and lit a new cigarette. 'You'd better fetch your conductor before it gets any warmer.' She took a long, deliberate drag and let it go without blowing, so that the smoke rose in a cluster to the zenith of the room. She bought organically grown cloves at the health-food store where she worked, rolling it into thin cigarettes, which she called lizard tails. 'C'mon,' she said, smiling falsely, 'go fetch.'

He considered telling her to go to hell but decided

it would only make things worse. 'That's OK,' he said, 'I think I'm cool enough now.'

'You're right,' she said, 'you don't look so hot anymore.'

She went over to the stack of boxes, picked up his beer, and tossed it to him. She opened a box marked 'A', for Annie, the name she insisted Frank call her because she thought her real name made her sound old and dreary. She withdrew an object wrapped in newspaper. 'The Black Bird,' she said, unveiling a teak salad bowl, and sat down on the floor in her taffeta dress. She spread out the newspaper at her feet and began painting her toenails the color of champagne. 'It's the horrorscope page,' she said. 'What sign were you born under?'

'A rock.'

'I'm serious, Richard.'

'That's why I'm laughing.'

She looked up at him as though she were reading a clock. 'Gemini, right?'

He popped open the beer.

'The twins,' she said, 'I should've known.' She squinted at the newspaper beneath her feet as if she were reading it. 'You will be the first person to have an orgasm in space.'

He looked at her expecting to see her smile at her own joke, but she kept a straight face as she daubed her nails with the little brush. He noticed for the first time that she was wearing a ring. 'And I wanted us to come at the same time,' he said.

She blew on her nails. 'Who said there'd be someone else?'

He turned and sat down on the windowsill so she wouldn't see him wince. He had been alone for some time now, and he was aware that his melancholy was hardening around him like a cocoon.

'Oh, I'm such a bitch,' she said, and she seemed genuinely sorry. 'It's just that I'm starving to death and Frank's probably at the Alibi right now drinking a greyhound and laughing at some retarded joke. I told him seven sharp. If he doesn't come in another ten minutes we'll just go ourselves and have a swell old time. What do you feel like eating? You're hungry, aren't you? You must be. I haven't eaten all day.'

She rummaged for something in her purse, a lipstick, and hoisted herself back up to the mirror. In the reflection she looked at Richard, who was looking out the window. The restaurant owner and a young guy Richard had never seen before were having a discussion in Italian, and by the looks of things, it was headed toward an argument.

'So how do I look?' Claire said, fluffing up her hair. 'Frank says I must've taken this dress off a dead person.'

'The ring,' Richard said. 'Did you take that off the same body?'

'I didn't have to *take* that,' Claire said quietly. 'A dead person *gave* that to me.' She turned the vertical knob on the TV, and the picture of a woman with very white teeth began to roll. 'It's not how things *look*, anyway,' she said and faced Richard, her wetly lipsticked mouth slightly opened like a fish's. 'Well, is she out there?'

Richard examined his beer can as if there were

something on it he hadn't read a hundred times before. 'I don't know who you're talking about,' he said. He was lying.

Claire smiled as if she had rehearsed it. 'You know,' she said, 'Isadora.'

That wasn't her real name, of course. None of them knew her real name. She was a waitress at Pinocchio's and probably not a day over seventeen. Frank was always saying that she was the sexiest girl he'd ever laid eyes on, though it was clear that the girl didn't comprehend her own beauty. And the funny thing was, Claire didn't seem to mind when Frank went on and on about the 'little meatball', as he called the girl. In fact, Claire would always embellish his descriptions, remarking on the girl's gorgeous hair, or the girl's sultry eyes, or the girl's magnificent chest, as if Claire somehow shared in Frank's lechery. It bothered Richard that he found himself excited when Claire said these things, the way she gave him that strange seductive look while brushing her breasts against his arm. Richard was afraid that Frank might notice, but he never did, or if he did it didn't seem to bother him.

'Let me get you a glass,' Claire said. She knew he didn't drink beer out of a glass. 'We just got new ones last weekend.'

Richard stared at the angry Italians beneath him, hoping they would come to blows. He thought it was typical of Claire to try pleasing him only to leave out some crucial detail, like putting the beer in the refrigerator. In this way, he could never really be satisfied, and yet he couldn't criticize her without sounding ungrateful. He wished they would just yell at each other, but he knew they wouldn't. You had to be lovers, Richard thought, or at least have been lovers once.

'Want another beer?' she asked. 'While I'm up, I mean.'

'No,' Richard said, his voice directed out the window. The Italians were shouting and waving their hands at each other, almost in cadence with the neon sign.

'Aw, c'mon,' Claire said. She took the empty can from Richard and walked into the kitchen. He looked after her. She had put on a lot of weight since she'd been with Frank and he was constantly reminding her of it. She came back with another beer and a glass, and when he reached out to take them from her, she moved past his hands and set them on his thighs.

'I shook it up,' Claire said. 'Do a shooter like we used to do in college.'

Richard looked at her but didn't say anything. He carefully peeled open the beer. Nothing happened. He looked at her again.

'So I didn't shake it up,' Claire said and laughed. 'You would've done it for Julie.' The harp had stopped playing upstairs. 'Where the hell is Frank, anyway?'

She bent over Richard and cupped her hands out the window as if to yell, but when she saw the Italians, she stepped back into the room. *Ollyollyoxenfree,* she said, staring into the carpet, and Richard stared at the same place, as if they believed Frank would actually emerge there.

'Remember that time outside the Rose,' Claire

said, 'when you ran up and hugged me, and you told me afterwards you thought I was Julie? You've got to remember this, because it's important to me.' But Richard couldn't recall. 'We'd been dancing for hours to that reggae band, and Julie was somewhere in the orchard taking a pee. I was pretty drunk and I wanted to take my mind off it, so I started counting between the lightning and the thunder – they weren't very far apart – and then these hands, your hands, wrap around me and pick me up, and I remember how scared I was until I saw it was you, your eyes closed and that big grin on your face. Like that was all you ever wanted out of life, to pick up your girl friend out in nowhere, to be drunk without a purpose in the rain.'

He wanted to turn away, but something in her gaze wouldn't let him. 'You knew it was me, didn't you?' Claire said. 'You knew it was me all along.'

'No,' Richard said, looking blank. 'I can't remember.'

She laughed nervously as the Italian voices surrounded them. 'Boy, they're really going at it, aren't they? I wonder what they're saying.'

'I don't speak Italian,' Richard said.

'Frank probably ran off with Isadora and this is her jealous boy friend come to find out what happened.'

'That must be it, Claire,' Richard said.

'Yeah, that must be it,' Claire said quietly, as if what she was saying were true.

She walked out of the open doorway to the bathroom down the hall, moving her hips like someone who knew she could be beautiful and just knowing was enough. Her long hair was bleached blond from too much sun and seemed to Richard to be very brittle. He had introduced Frank and Claire at a potluck back when Frank was Richard's boss at Social Security, and Claire told Richard later that she was very attracted to Frank, swearing Richard to secrecy. A couple of days later Claire came up in conversation and Richard asked Frank what he had thought of her. Frank said she seemed like a stupid surfer chick, a real airhead, so Richard never mentioned her again. In six months Frank and Claire were a couple, and Claire told Richard she was surprised he had kept their secret, that Frank hadn't known she was after him. It had made Richard and Claire closer, but Richard had only kept his mouth shut because he thought Frank didn't like her; he would have told him otherwise.

Outside, the owner was really pissed off now, saying the young guy's name over and over very slowly, like a little kid practicing a cuss word. 'Gino,' he said. 'Gino, Gino, Gino.' The young guy just stood there about to cry. Richard recognized the tightness in his jaw, and found his own jaw becoming rigid. The telephone rang five times before he answered it.

'Hello?' Richard said.

'Is this Pinocchio's?' a man's voice asked. He was either high or drunk or both. Richard could tell it was Frank disguising his voice.

'I'd like to order a family with everything on it,' Frank said, 'with extra anchovies, please.' There were some girls laughing in the background. It

98

sounded as though he were calling from a video arcade.

'I think you have the wrong number,' Richard said.

'Oh no, this is the right number,' Frank said. 'This number is so right I could shit.'

There was a pause. Then Frank laughed again and the girls laughed with him. And then all Richard could hear was the electronic beeps and explosions from the video games.

'I hope you're enjoying my wife,' Frank said in his normal voice. 'I hope she dances for you before she takes it off.'

Richard didn't say anything.

Frank hung up.

When Richard turned to get his beer, Claire was standing in the doorway looking past him out the window. The Italians were no longer there. 'Who was on the phone?' she asked.

'Wrong number,' Richard said.

'Whoever it was must've had something interesting to say.'

'He was wasted,' Richard said. 'I couldn't understand a word he said.'

'Was it Frank?' she asked with not enough inflection.

'I don't think so,' he said, 'not so you could recognize him anyway.'

'Well, when is he coming home?'

There was a stillness then, as if they could say something to each other they had never said before. Richard got up from the couch and went to the mirror. Normally when he'd been drinking he avoided mirrors – there was nothing more depressing than to see yourself alone at a bar in a wall-sized mirror – but right now he needed to know what he was feeling.

'Why didn't you tell me?' he said with his back to her. 'Why didn't you tell me you married him?'

He looked in the mirror, but didn't see himself, only the reflection of Claire's puffy, made-up face. She didn't say anything for the longest time, and when she finally began speaking, it was in the voice of someone in an emergency, calm yet freighted with emotion.

'Oh Jesus,' she said, 'we had a little wine, you know? We were watching some stupid program, some police-show crap, and Frank starts getting affectionate. I promised him I only slept with Chris the one time, and he believed me, Richard. We were feeling pretty good about things, you know? And then he says out of nowhere, let's get married. Let's drive to Reno tonight. We've got time, he says – it seemed like the right thing, that's all. We got a nice room cheap in a little town on the Truckee River, I forget the name. It was real nice, Richard. A little post office, wooden sidewalks, stuff like that. Real romantic, you know, out by the river and everything. Frank even got this little girl to hold the Instamatic while we posed. The best picture we ever took. I was in love with him and he was in love with me. We sang "You Ought to Be in Pictures" all the way home, and the Fiat only heated up once.'

Claire shielded her eyes with her hand as if she were staring into a bright light or the sun. 'But when we got back it was the same between us, the same as it was before we left.'

Richard studied her for a while and wasn't sure if she was crying, and then, just as it seemed she would collapse, he went to her and they embraced and they began to slowly turn as if the harp were still playing and this were a dance. They were alone in that little room and they knew it, and they knew they would be alone for as far ahead as they could see and they were going to make the best of it. It all came back to Richard in a hurry: the inexorable breath, the vining touch, this quiet sinking into love, and he found himself whispering, not so she could hear, 'I remember. I remember.'

Outside Isadora was on her break now, sitting alone on an empty milk case and smoking a cigarette that lit up her cheeks. Richard could see her as he turned and she was more beautiful than he remembered, and he imagined her on bicycles, imagined her in dresses, imagined her in winter rooms with sweeping vistas, lost in his arms instead of Claire. She was prettier than Julie, he thought, she was prettier.

THE ARTICHOKE LEAGUE

TV Guide said it would happen and it did: *The Fugitive* came back on today. I wrote the station a letter when they took it off the air. That was back in December, on my thirtieth birthday. I blew out the candles on the key-lime pie that my mother, Sylvia, bakes for me every year and made my wish out loud. 'Please bring back *The Fugitive*,' I said. Sylvia was sitting across the card table from me in her aqua satin party dress, looking like I'd just taken a swing at her. A pretty young wife with her own transportation. A teller's job at B of A. That's what Sylvia wishes I'd wish for. But I got out the tablet instead and wrote my letter. Sylvia is always threatening to write a letter to the TV for one reason or another, but I actually did it. She says I need to take the initiative more. Now that I have, what can she say?

Plenty, as it turns out. She's pounding on the ceiling below me with the toilet end of a plumber's helper. 'Walter,' she's yelling, 'Walter, CAN YOU HEAR ME?' I've got the Walkman set on 7 with the TV three quarters of the way up and I can still hear her. 'Walter,' she yells, 'are you ready? ARE YOU REH-DEE?'

103

I take a last hit off the roach I'm smoking and grind it into the Coast League Champs trophy that I won in the fifth grade. I'm sorry to report that the One-Armed Man isn't on this episode of The Fugitive. I can tell within the first five minutes if he's going to be on, that's how many times I've seen these shows. I press the OFF button on the remote and watch the screen go black.

The One-Armed Man is the guy who really should've been taking the rap all along, the guy The Fugitive is always chasing while the cops chase him. It's funny because I can't exactly remember what The Fugitive supposedly did, just that everybody is chasing everybody else, and that they're all so certain about who's guilty. That's what I like about the One-Armed Man. He knows what he did and he doesn't get hemorrhoids about it.

Sylvia could learn a few lessons from his character, but she won't look at The Fugitive. She says it's morbid that I like this show. Because why? I ask her, and then she clams up. Because I'm a One-Armed Man too. I was also a One-Armed Boy, though I didn't begin life that way. I lost my arm in the same accident that I lost my father. We were on our way back from my second no-hitter, the game that clinched the county championship in '74. My father was listening to scores on the car radio – Giants over Pittsburgh, two-to-one in ten – and he was humming, which he never did, and I was looking at the back of his neck – he'd just gotten a haircut and you know the way a haircut makes your neck stand out – and Sylvia was sitting in the seat beside him staring out the window into a garlic field.

104

Then boom, this picker runs a stop and broadsides us. Sylvia thinks he did it on purpose, that the picker had this death wish or something. The CHP found a half-eaten tamale next to the picker's body on the seat of his flatbed. What kind of guy kills himself while he's eating a tamale?

Sylvia's pounding on the ceiling again. 'Walter,' she yells, 'are you happy? ARE YOU HEAH-PEE?'

I turn the set back on and close my eyes. 'I want to understand you,' a woman is saying to The Fugitive. 'You will in time,' The Fugitive tells her. 'May I use your car?'

I'm a shade between animal and vegetable. That's the first thing I tell Sylvia when I get in the Chevette, that and how I'm bigger than a breadbox and a whole lot meaner. Then I tell her to ask me the other eighteen questions.

Sylvia doesn't say anything, though. Just sits there like a June bug with its wings torn off, looking in the rearview at God knows what, oil stains, maybe, in the back of the garage. Sylvia warms up the Chevette for fifteen minutes just so we can go on the ten-minute ride to El Nido Park. For someone who has to know everything she sure doesn't know very much.

'So you've got what you need then,' Sylvia says finally, meaning my chest protector and my mask and, most important, the safety pin she sets out for me before every game so I can pin up my sleeve.

I nod yes and off we go, the Chevette pinging from the regular Sylvia buys at 7-Eleven. It doesn't hit me until a mile later that she managed to ask me a question without it being a question, which really pisses me off. I crank up the radio, this somebody-done-somebody-wrong crap that Sylvia always has on, and punch the KRMA ('Hits that get back at you') button. Then I wait for Sylvia to ask me real polite if maybe I could turn it down.

It was a hippie girl who lived behind El Nido Park that first turned me on to KRMA, back when KRMA was still psychedelic and I still thought you could make it to the Bigs with only one arm, the way Pete Gray made it in the forties when all the whole players were still fighting the war. She had long red hair and wore kimonos, and sometimes she'd do the pharaoh dance on her back porch where everybody at El Nido could see, right after somebody's kid got a bases-loaded triple, or somebody's kid fell off the score-board, or somebody's kid did anything to get the crowd stirred up. She'd never do it when I asked her to, though, which I counted as a sign we would never be lovers, and I was right. She kissed me one time is all, and that was when I told her that the day I lost my arm was the day I stopped taking things for granted, the day I realized what a privilege it is to play mumblety-peg or carry block ice to a cooler.

Her father worked at Parks and Rec, and he got me the job as homeplate umpire (the job I hold today) in the little leagues down at El Nido – she used to say it the right way, the Spanish way, El Needo. It meant 'The Need', she said. It was what people needed, it was what *I* needed, because I always had this hangdog expression on my face. I never told her that El Nido really means 'The Nest', or how Frank Jarvis got stabbed to death in the parking lot at El Nido in the middle of a Canners'

League game. I had no intention of putting a crimp in her pharaoh dancing. She had the best handjive I've ever seen.

'You're out on the streets looking good,' Janis is singing on the radio, like old times, when Sylvia reaches over and snaps it off. 'If you have to smoke marijuana, I wish you wouldn't do it in my house,' she says. She's looking out at the road, but I can tell she's watching me in her peripheral vision. 'I'd rather not be put in jail at this point in my life, thank you. What will I say to the police if they come to the door?'

'Tell them I have glaucoma.'

'I don't know what makes you think you can umpire effectively when you take drugs,' she says, all excited now. 'I'm surprised you can even find homeplate, let alone balls and strikes.' She puts on her left-turn blinker even though we're still a half mile from Las Cruces Street. It's a right on Las Cruces through Pickertown to El Nido.

'At least I know where the ball park is,' I say. A left on Las Cruces takes you up to Route 6, the intersection where my father was killed. Sylvia hasn't gone up there since the accident, not with me in the car, anyway. The sound from the blinker is giving me a headache. I wipe saliva on my temples and roll down my window.

'We have to pick up Carl Winslow,' Sylvia says. 'His mother called and said she couldn't get off work today for the game. She said half the staff at the Ramada is out with the flu.'

I stick my arm out the window as far as it will go. A crane fly splats against my palm. 'Yeah, the male half. And she's the one who gave it to them.' I turn and give Sylvia the dogeye. 'Only I wouldn't call it the flu.'

Sylvia switches the radio back on, but the volume is so low you can only hear the bass. For a while it's in concert with the blinker. 'Marijuana must give a person startling insights,' she says. 'I feel privileged that you're willing to share them with an unenlightened person like me.' She switches the radio off again. 'And could you please roll up that window? I've got the AC on.'

I close my fist around the crane fly and squeeze. I can't feel anything. 'I've got another joint in my wallet,' I say, staring out the window. 'I'd be willing to share that with you, too.' In the field beyond, a man is burning some trash in an oil drum with his hands out over the fire. It's like he's trying to stay warm when it must be eighty degrees outside. I push the cigarette lighter in on the dashboard. 'How about it?' I say.

But Sylvia is serious about her driving now. Her hands are gnarled around the steering wheel and her long body is sitting bolt-upright in the seat. She lifts her foot off the accelerator and lets the car take itself up to the intersection, to the sign for Route 6 and the stop sign, plain as day, that the picker never saw. There're some rows of corn now where there used to be strawberries, and in the garlic field there's an oil pump with a big toothy grin painted on it, clanging like a flagpole in the wind. Besides that everything's the same. No skid marks, no safety glass, no blood. No sign that anything good or bad ever happened here. It makes you wonder how many places like it there are in the world, dumb little places where people's lives were changed forever, places you pass by every day without once taking notice.

Sylvia peers around me down the highway. The road's straight as an arrow in either direction and there's not a trace of tule fog; the visibility's perfect. 'Is it clear?' Sylvia asks and smiles sweetly, though without looking in my direction. 'Please tell me when it's clear, Walter.'

I rub the seat where my missing arm should be resting. 'It's clear,' I say.

The cigarette lighter pops out, giving Sylvia a start. She holds her hand flat against her collarbone. 'Please check again, Walter. For me.'

Sylvia was born without depth perception, meaning she can only see in two dimensions. I'm convinced my father didn't know that when he married her or he wouldn't have gone through with it – she might've passed that gene on to me, and you can't hit a fastball without seeing depth. I did inherit Sylvia's tallness, however, which I know was according to my father's plan. He'd spent six years with the Dodger farm club in Lodi as a catcher (hit for average, good defense), but the scouts finally told him he needed five inches and some power to make it to the majors and they sent him home.

He met Sylvia a short time later in Topeka, Kansas, where I was born. By the time I was six, we had moved to California so I could play baseball year round. At twelve I was the starting left fielder for the Babe Ruth League Champion Badgers. At thirteen I won the batting crown, second in HR's and

109

Ribbies. My father didn't convert me into a pitcher until I was in high school, and even then he wouldn't let me throw the curve. He'd heard all kinds of stories about kids who'd wrecked their arms throwing a breaking pitch too young, and after all, Drysdale's father never let Donny throw the curve.

I never played a single inning at El Nido Park until the accident; it was literally on the other side of the tracks. That's where pickers and canners played, where transients used dope and exposed themselves. Me and my buddies made jokes about it, but really we were scared. Our teams played in clean ball parks with flush toilets and concession stands. We had fancy uniforms with our names stitched on back; we had cheerleaders; we had mothers. Our fathers took us out for pizza when we won. Our losses were few and far between.

'It's clear,' I say, looking out onto the highway again. I shade my eyes with my hand for emphasis. 'Really,' I say, 'you can go now if you want.'

Carl Winslow, a.k.a. The Sidewinder, is sitting out front in his Solon uniform next to some metal trash cans. His address is painted on the trash cans with red fingernail polish, 203 #A; 203 #B is rented to a biker. Usually he's out in the driveway working on his Triumph, but today I don't see him or his bike. He must have the flu, too.

I get out of the front seat and let The Sidewinder ride shotgun. I figure he needs a mother more than I do. Plus I like the idea of Sylvia chauffeuring me around. All of this is done without a word. The Sidewinder's afraid of me because I only have the one arm.

'Well, don't you look sharp in your uniform,' Sylvia says once we've crossed Route 6 again.

It takes a while for The Sidewinder to figure out she's talking to him. 'Thank you, Mrs Crenshaw,' he says, sitting up straighter.

'You must be excited about the game,' Sylvia says and shoots me a you-should-be-giving-him-advice glare in the rearview. 'I know Walter is.'

'The Sidewinder doesn't get too excited about baseball, do you, Sidewinder?'

'I guess not, Mr Crenshaw.'

'He was until you said that to him,' Sylvia says.

'Is that right, Sidewinder? Were you excited before I said that to you?'

He takes off his cap, exposing little tufts of chartreuse hair, and for the first time I notice that he's got a stud in his ear. Sylvia must be having a cow. 'I guess not, Mr Crenshaw,' he says.

'You don't have to answer his questions if you don't want to, Carl,' Sylvia says, quietly. 'That's part of free speech – no speech at all.'

'I know, Mrs Crenshaw,' he says.

I lean over the seat. 'Put on the radio, if you want, Sidewinder. Anything you like.' And he promptly dials in this really rude rock 'n'roll, fuzz guitar and witch lyrics, music to commit mayhem by. 'Go ahead, turn it up,' I say and remove my wallet from my shirt pocket. I take out the crumpled joint from between two ones and stick it in my mouth. 'Would you push that lighter in for me, Sidewinder. I'd very much appreciate it.'

111

Sylvia's really mad-dogging me in the rearview now. 'I hope you're not going to smoke in the car, Walter,' she practically shouts above the radio. 'I may be a goner, but I wish you'd consider this *young* person's lungs.'

The lighter pops out and The Sidewinder hands it back to me without being asked. 'See, he doesn't mind,' I say and push the red metal coil onto the joint. I take a good hit. It's raspy.

'He's too *young* to know what's good for him,' Sylvia says.

Well, you're too *old* to know what's good for you, I start to say. But I don't. Some things are better thought than said, especially in the company of your mother.

Sylvia cuts in front of a garbage truck and passes a candy-apple red Impala on the right. Everybody drives slow in Pickertown – it's like the getting-there is more important than the destination, or the place they're starting from. The drive through Pickertown is why Sylvia didn't want to run the new concession stand at El Nido to begin with, but I finally convinced her to take the job. It's really no big deal, just throw the dogs in the microwave, make sure the Heath Bars stay out of the sun. It took a while, but now she's really into it, all the corny rules they have and everything. For instance, when you're on the winning team, you get some grape Sno-Kone syrup in a Dixie cup, no ice, compliments of El Nido Park (the only reason it's grape is because no one ever buys that flavor). If you're on the losing team, you have to buy your own Sno-Kone; Sylvia won't give you the syrup in a cup, even if you're willing to pay extra. I gave The Sidewinder a Lincoln one time to bribe her with, but she wouldn't go for it. Sylvia says you have to win.

The Chevette is filled up with marijuana smoke now. Sylvia slides off the AC and rolls her window all the way down. The resultant breeze extinguishes my joint. But I act like it's still going anyway. I wouldn't want to give Sylvia any satisfaction.

By the time we get to El Nido, it's still an hour before game time and no one else is there. The Sidewinder is sitting in the Solon dugout staring out at me while I chalk the foul lines, though he turns away every time I look in his direction. Sylvia's in the concession stand popping corn.

Here at El Nido, we play good old-fashioned country hardball as my father used to call it. No tee-ball. No metal bats. No spikes. Four balls to a walk, three strikes to a *K*, three outs to an inning. We play six innings or until it gets dark, whichever comes first, unless, of course, we're into the play-offs like we are now, and then we play the full six even if we have to pick it up the next day. Extra innings are the same deal. The only other wrinkle in the rules has to do with the train, which runs beyond the outfield fence, from the NO EXPECTORATING sign in left, past the bill-board for Bucky's Bait and Tackle in right. It doesn't say anything about trains in the rulebook, but I always stop play anyhow, wait until the thing rattles by on its way to Wyoming or wherever the hell trains go. We don't have an organist or a seventh-inning stretch at El Nido. We have a train.

113

'You forgot something,' Sylvia says, tapping me on the shoulder.

It's the safety pin, new and shiny, resting in her outstretched hand. I glare at her but she won't budge.

'Let me put it on for you,' she says.

I'm dreaming strike *tres* – this little dove floating down the pipe while the hitter just stands there, it's such a thing of beauty – when The Sidewinder lets go of another tight one and Rosalita gets pancaked for the third pitch in a row. The boos are really coming now. It's two out in the sixth with the game tied 18 to 18 and a runner on at first. It wouldn't be so bad except the crowd's eighty percent Mexican and they don't see how a big white kid like The Sidewinder can be throwing at their Rosalita when it's her first season in the Artichoke League and The Sidewinder's been around for what seems like forever. And damn if Gordon's not up there in the announcer's booth slurping into the microphone about brush-back pitches and crosstown rivalries when really these teams are a bunch of nine-year-olds who play this game because their folks say they have to.

Rosalita stares up at me from her seat in the batter's box, pleading with her baby-brown *ojos*. I take off my mask and give Gordon the cut sign as I head for the mound. I feel sorry for The Sidewinder (though officially I'm impartial) because I know he's always been wild and never meant to throw at anybody in his life. This could very well be his last game in the Artichoke League. He'll be eleven in September and that's the age cutoff and it's a disgrace to make it to the Coast League by default – his buddies all made it in the tryouts last year. But sometimes in the interest of riot control these warnings are necessary, especially during the playoffs. It doesn't really matter, anyway – even wasted pickers are afraid to hit a cripple.

Which might lead you to wonder how a person with one arm can be an umpire, even if it is in a Little League in a fourth-rate ball park like El Nido. You might wonder if, when he gives the safe sign on a close play, he loses his balance, starts spinning like a compass in a roomful of magnets. I know I had those kinds of morbid curiosities before I lost my arm; I always wanted to know what blind people see when they come. But, if you think about it, I bet you don't know what you see when you come. I certainly don't. It's just the kind of half-thought I had about blind people before I lost my – it cracks me up the way when somebody's finger gets chopped off or their eye gets poked people always say, 'Chet lost a finger,' or 'Ginger lost an eye,' like someday they might find it under the cushions on the divan with their missing car keys. I can just see Sylvia waving my mangled arm in my face, saying in that babytalk voice she gets, 'If it'd been a snake, it would've bit you.' She still talks about the day my father was *lost* as though he took the wrong exit off the highway and came home fifteen minutes late. My father was never lost a day in his life. That's what got him killed more than anything.

When I get to the mound, The Sidewinder is kicking away the dirt on the backside of the rubber. He must've seen a pitcher do that on TV.

'Sidewinder,' I say, 'you're out of control out here.'

115

He stops kicking the dirt and looks out toward right field. He must've seen that on TV, too. 'I know, Mr Crenshaw,' he says.

'Maybe you're just trying too hard.' I make an effort to imagine what my father would've told me in this situation, but it's inconceivable. I was never allowed to get myself into a jam like this. 'Just throw it down the middle,' I say. 'Just let her hit it.'

He looks at me directly for the first time this afternoon. 'Was that marijuana you were smoking in the car today?'

'No,' I tell him.

'My mother use to smoke marijuana, but I got her to quit. It's not very good for you, Mr Crenshaw.' He hands me his glove with the baseball tucked inside. 'You shouldn't do things that aren't good for you,' he says. And then he walks off the field. He doesn't even go to his dugout, just hops the fence by third base and disappears into the crowd.

Everybody is cheering now, this crazy high wail of a cheer like it's the first time in their lives they ever got what they wanted. But then, just as quick, they stop, like maybe they didn't really want what they asked for after all. I turn, dropping Sidewinder's glove, and fold my arm over my chest protector as though I had two, and stare out past left field where my hippie friend once did her handjive. I never wanted that train to come by more than I do right now, but there's something missing in my wish, like when I get wasted and spend my whole disability on Lotto tickets – I know it won't come true.

I crane my neck upward and see the sky blue and

cloudless above, with three hours left of daylight in it, and when I turn back and stare down at home-plate, I see Sylvia standing behind the chain-link backstop with her fingers curled around the mesh. I can tell that she's praying, but for a change it doesn't make me mad. It seems like it's the good kind of praying, the kind she used to do when I was still pitching and she wanted things to go right, instead of later on after the accident, when she prayed for things not to go wrong. It's the perfect moment to call off the game, and when I try to raise my left arm to do just that, I realize that it's the arm in the ground someplace, in the place where they bury all the severed parts, and it makes me bust out laughing because I haven't made that mistake in a long, long time. A flicker of smile crosses Sylvia's face now, and I get that feeling you get when you're walking down the street thinking something that tickles you, and you look up and see a stranger grinning right along with you. I swear the whole crowd is grinning, too, and so is the Solon bench, as I walk off the field through their dugout with the score even into perpetuity, or at least until the commissioner can find my replacement.

Sylvia and Sidewinder are waiting side by side in the front seat when I get to the car, and without thinking I tell them to scoot over and then sit myself behind the wheel. I've watched Sylvia do it a million times, so when I start the Chevette and put it in drive, it's like I'm acting out of habit, instead of doing it for the first time. My foot eases down the accelerator and the car pulls us out onto the road, and for once I'm grateful that Las Cruces is as straight as the earth it's paved on, grateful that it leads out of town to nowhere, where the dirt is hard and full of clay, where only sagebrush and foxtails are able to take hold. Sylvia and Sidewinder are staring out the windshield at the same flat horizon, but you can tell their minds are going in a hundred different directions. As for me, I can't help wondering what Sylvia did back at the concession stand. Did she set out the grape syrup in Dixie cups and just leave it there for whoever wanted it? For guys who've never ever been to El Nido before, who don't know about the rules, about the winners and the losers, guys off the street with an ordinary thirst?

I let go of the wheel and take my foot off the accelerator, but Sylvia doesn't say anything and neither does Sidewinder. The car drifts on course for a little while and then, as it loses speed, veers off onto the shoulder, where it stops against a white wooden post bearing a speed-limit sign. The car idles for a little bit and then stalls for no good reason.

I look over at the both of them: Sylvia's stretching and Sidewinder's yawning, as though we've been driving for hours now without a rest.

'Don't you want to know where we're going?' I ask, and my voice as I say it sounds high and funny.

Sylvia looks at me and then turns the rearview so she can look at herself. 'Seems like we already got there,' she says.

'Yeah,' Sidewinder says and nods his chartreuse head. 'We're here.'

THE CAMERA

Phillip remembers very clearly the night he met her. It was on the subway, the last train back from the city, and they were both very drunk, at least she says she was drunk, though now he has reason to disbelieve her. She boarded the train alone and sat down next to a large black man who was wearing a yellow plastic raincoat. Phillip remembers thinking that she looked very pretty, though he also remembers thinking that she looked full of herself. The train pulled out of the station and she put a cigarette in her mouth, a Salem, and was fumbling in her purse for a match. The man sitting next to her lit her cigarette with a disposable lighter and then calmly returned the lighter, along with his hand, to his coat pocket.

Phillip watched the entire sequence from his seat across from them. After she had taken a few drags, she looked directly at the place where Phillip was sitting and said: 'This is a movie. The man sitting next to me represents Humphrey Bogart and I represent Lauren Bacall. We have never met before, but we will leave this train hand in hand and make passionate love through the night and into tomorrow.

119

This is a movie because things like this only happen in movies, and I want them to happen to me.'

The man looked at her nervously but didn't say anything, and when the train came to the next station, he got off without her, shaking his head. Phillip remembers the way she looked at that moment, like a child who, having done herself some minor harm, waits for an audience before acknowledging the pain. When she was still crying through the next two stations, Phillip went to her and consoled her, though he can't remember what he said to make her feel better. At her apartment, she prepared him peppermint tea, and he realized for the first time that she was quite a bit older than he was. She explained that she had just moved away from her boy friend and that she was planning to have many spontaneous sexual affairs. Phillip spent the night on the futon in her living room.

Now, five months later, Phillip considers that night a revelation, unlike the steady blur of events that have proceeded from his moving in with her. With Rebecca, he says out loud. He is trying to become more personable. It is 3 a.m. and they have just made love, and he is sitting at her butcher-block table reading Dear Abby. He rarely reads Dear Abby, particularly at 3 a.m., but then he rarely makes love, a fact that once troubled him but no longer seems to – now he is more worried about his stoicism than having a regular sex life.

Rebecca is in the other room dreaming. Phillip knows she is dreaming because he waited until she fell asleep and then watched as her eyes swirled beneath her lids. Phillip tries to remember his dreams but can't. He envies her because she always remembers her dreams and recounts them vividly in what he considers a little girl's voice. They are very pleasant dreams, her dreams. His dreams on the other hand usually end violently and involve faceless assailants. Often he wakes up shouting, sometimes running naked to her kitchen. He has told her that they are cat dreams, that they involve making cat love, stalking cat prey, but this is a lie. She smiles in her dreams, he thinks. She smiles while my throat is being cut.

There are several letters in Dear Abby, but the one from Going Crazy sticks in Phillip's mind. A desperate mother has overheard her thirteen-year-old daughter saying that she would do anything the nineteen-year-old boy next door asked her to. The mother is convinced that this includes sexual favors and she is praying that her daughter will save herself for marriage. Abby tells the woman that while prayer is wonderful it certainly isn't a contraceptive. Phillip is bothered by this advice; Rebecca doesn't use any birth control as far as he can tell, and the one time he surprised her with a condom, she turned over on her side of the bed and wouldn't have sex with him for a week. Phillip is not a religious person. He has never been to church in his life, except for a few weddings and his grandmother's funeral. He wishes that there were a picture of Going Crazy so that he could see if she was really worried or if she was merely a puritanical fool.

After all, he, Phillip, is not married to Rebecca. He doesn't even have a picture of her! He asked her for one once, but she said she didn't have any. She didn't keep pictures of anyone, she told him. Phillip has many pictures. Of women. He looks at the pictures when he masturbates, which is often. The women are naked (of course, he thinks) but the expressions on their faces seem to mask boredom or fatigue. There are usually blurbs about the models – their names, ages, occupations, where they are from, what they like men and/or women to do to them. But he knows they are lies because he has seen the same models in other magazines and they have different names, different desires.

He goes to her room and watches her, sitting on a stool by the open window. At dawn, her cat gets a bird, a black-throated sparrow.

The next day is Sunday and when he wakes up he is in her bed alone. She has cleaned up the feathers from the bird and the cat has been put outside, the window closed. He tries to remember the day she asked him to move in with her but can't. He thinks it was a Sunday and that her reasons were practical.

He starts by checking her filing cabinet, which is unlocked. Then he spills the drawers from her dresser onto her bed. He goes through the clothes in her closet and checks under the sink in the bathroom. He dumps the contents of her hope chest over a pile of *Glamour* magazines. Nothing. No pictures. In an envelope taped under a drawer in her desk, he finds a package of birth-control pills, unopened. There is also a bill from a plastic surgeon detailing the charges from a breast-implant operation. He tries to remember what he knows about her. She is

122

thirty-five. She works at a department store. She has a predilection for chocolate and cats. He has never touched another woman's breasts and now he wonders if his experience has been in any way genuine. On his eighteenth birthday, after an uneventful childhood, his parents told him that he was adopted. They told him while he was still eating his cake! He tries to imagine how he felt then and compares it to how he feels now. He wants to experience a sad déjà vu.

When she gets home he begins yelling at her, something he has never done before. How can anyone not have pictures, everybody has pictures, I'm going to take your goddamn picture and blow it up the size of this wall (he points to the wall). What do you think about that? he asks her. Everybody has a goddamn past, he says. She doesn't say anything. She is still holding the groceries, with an expression like she has just walked into the wrong apartment. He has his hand in his pants and he is holding himself. She walks calmly into her bedroom and when she emerges again she is wearing a paisley scarf over her mouth. She says something in a low voice that he can't make out. She says it again without raising her voice: she will have him arrested if he doesn't leave within the next five minutes.

Phillip's parents live in Roanoke, Virginia. He hasn't seen them in two years. He is tempted to call his mother, to tell her what has just happened to him, but he thinks it will be difficult to explain. The woman I live with has artificial breasts. He doesn't like the way this sounds. He has never spoken very

123

easily to his mother about sex. Besides, he thinks, this is a pay phone.

The motel he chooses is very clean, with a satellite dish displayed prominently on the roof of the office. He stays up late watching one-star movies. He has always been a fan of Howard Duff and Ida Lupino. He calls Rebecca several times, making sure to hang up in mid-ring. Now her line is busy. He calls the newspaper on the outside chance he can leave an empathetic message for Going Crazy. A woman answers and for a moment he is convinced that he's dialed the wrong number, that he's speaking to Rebecca. 'I can see you,' he says and holds the telephone up to the picture tube: a pretty young actress is explaining the virtues of Boraxo to a Russian wolfhound.

In the morning he dials his number at the insurance-claims office where he works. The receptionist answers and he tells her that he's contracted sugar diabetes. In the five years that he has worked there, he has never called in sick before. At noon he checks out of the motel and drives to the mall, to the department store where Rebecca is employed. He takes the escalator past the Cosmetics Department (without seeing Rebecca) to the high-tech basement. He explains to the clerk, a woman, that he needs the movie camera to objectify his life. Women have always confided in him easily before Rebecca. Women have changed clothes in front of him without even flinching. You never had sex with any of these women, Phillip reminds himself. The clerk seems to recognize Phillip. It is as though he is a felon trying to purchase a gun. 'Cash or charge?'

the clerk says, pressing an intricate series of buttons. Rebecca, Phillip says inwardly, and hands her his orange-and-yellow credit card.

He considers the sinister ramifications of his behavior. This is in the department-store restaurant and he has just ordered a Cobb salad. There are women all around him, women who seem to be suffering the effects of leisure time. He is quite distressed himself. There has never been a crime perpetrated with a camera. He repeats this. He remembers a conversation he overheard once at an office party. An older man was telling a younger woman that a snuff movie had been shown across the street from the White House. Phillip remembers that the woman looked quite drawn. In a light-hearted voice, the man told the woman that if she ever saw one she would laugh at how fake everything looked, this fake blood spurting all over the place. Phillip wonders if the man had actually seen a snuff movie or if he had merely read about one someplace. 'Here you go,' the waitress says and sets the salad down in front of Phillip. He is certain she knows that he's been staring at her. 'Would you like cracked pepper?' she says, her lips slightly parting as she waits for his reply.

He considers the fact that he is in love with her. With *Rebecca*, he says out loud. This option has always seemed improbable before now, for such a calculating individual as himself. But seeing her through a camera has brought him closer to her. The camera has a zoom lens and he can be close to her from great distances. He can watch her movements without their corresponding sounds and this sensory pureness is cathartic. He can know now what he feels for her and it is a deep and unfathomable love.

But this is all part of his imagination, an imagination that is moving him toward action, toward tranquillity and death. The camera is still in the box and he is frantically reading the directions behind a rack of corduroy suits. The directions seem to have been written in another language and then translated into English. Words are misspelled, sentences grammatically flawed. He has never been technically inclined and the department store will be closing in another half hour. This is simply not enough time to master the subtle workings of this device, he thinks, this camera of which I am now the owner. He peeks his head above the corduroy suits. Rebecca is shutting down her cash register early, for a reason quite inexplicable to Phillip. He watches her present the cash drawer to her supervisor and then watches as she says something perfunctory and, judging by her supervisor's face, satisfactory. She leans down and withdraws her purse from a space beneath the counter. She is wearing the paisley scarf around her neck. He follows her at a safe distance to Linens, noticing a slight hitch in her walk. He wonders if he is in any way responsible, if there is such a thing as hysterical lameness. He suddenly remembers the camera, which he has tucked under his arm, and just as quickly tries to forget it. He doubts if he would understand this movie any better if he ever saw it again.

In Sporting Goods, she buys a blue leather softball glove and a blue aluminum bat, talking amiably to the sales clerk, with whom she seems familiar. Phillip has never known Rebecca to be athletic, a fact that melds into the feelings of sorrow and detachment that he keeps for Rebecca, the Sporting Goods Department, the department store, the mall at large. He is squatting behind a life-size cutout of Kareem Abdul-Jabbar. He imagines whole and subsidiary branches of Rebecca's life that she has concealed from him, seemingly without effort. Pockets of information stashed like Easter eggs in nooks and crannies throughout her apartment, only to be unearthed by future archeologists who will piece together what he will never piece together, who will nod solemnly at a calamity Phillip never foresaw, like a diner at a Vesuvian table.

The lights in the department store flash on and off several times, signaling to Phillip that the grim and monotonous events of his life are about to resume. He follows Rebecca to the Toy Department, where she buys several stuffed animals, an Etch A Sketch, a nightlight in the shape of Garfield the Cat. He looks up at a video camera, which is pointed at the aisle where he is walking. He is no longer making an effort to conceal himself. He is convinced that she is aware of him, but that it is an awareness she will never acknowledge, like an actress trained to disavow the camera that is filming her. He is convinced that what he is seeing is what the department-store cameras are seeing, that his eyes are attached to a cable that is attached to a monitor in a dim little room where a dim little man is watching. He can see himself as this man. He can see himself as the man who is watching what he sees!

He is directly behind her now. He is following Rebecca up the escalator to God knows where. Her arms are full of packages that in toto are larger than herself. She needs to drop ballast or she will never complete this ascent. He wants to want to help her. She is practically tripping backward and the use of her hands is not available to her. He imagines the stuffed animals free-falling into Men's Furnishings. He imagines the baseball bat crashing through a glass case full of eelskin wallets. He imagines the air around them thinning, that they are climbing to an uninhabitable plane far above the clouds.

But really it's the third floor, a truth pronounced by a large 3 painted on the wall facing the escalator. Rebecca makes it to the candy counter intact and orders a quarter pound of orange slices from a sandy-haired adolescent, who benignly honors her request. On the PA, a woman's voice is reminding shoppers to make their final purchases, that the department store will be closing in another five minutes. He is standing immediately in front of her as she crams wedge after wedge into her little mouth, as she stares through him at a display of ladies' designer watches and matching designer luggage. Bits of orange gum arabic are sticking on her teeth and he is powerless to stop it. He can only record the inevitable.

In Maternity, she moves quickly to her size on a rack of blouses and picks up one of the hangers in her teeth. He follows her into a dressing room, where she collapses on the little bench amid a fortress of consumer goods. Now she is undressing and he is sitting in her place on the bench. Now she has removed her pastel cotton sweater and is unbuttoning her pastel cotton shirt. Now she is naked from the waist up. Now she is wearing a size-ten smock with little magicians pulling little rabbits out of little top hats. She looks down at him, at his pudgy pink face, at his unwitting innocence and kindness. She carefully removes the camera from his lap and sits herself across his thighs.

'Cheese,' she says, and Phillip's life, to his chagrin, does not flash before his eyes; it is instead proceeding from this moment forward at its usual blinding speed. He looks out across Rebecca's shoulder (she is kissing him on the neck), out over the wooden saloon doors of the dressing room, out past Maternity and Nightwear and Hosiery, where a product housed in plastic eggs is revolving on a secret axis. He is watching an older couple recede from him gracefully toward the nether region of the department store. They are not touching each other, but he can see, even at this distance, that they are intimate, that they are synchronized in a way that is beyond even their understanding. The man is balding and stoop-shouldered and the woman is thin and slightly pigeon-toed. Their physiques are a description of himself, and he realizes without flinching that these are his parents, his natural parents, and that they have come shopping in this store, at this hour, by accident, in the very fashion that they have brought him to this world. He watches as they leave, first the department store, then the mall, as they seat themselves in their modest automobile, as they negotiate on-ramps and off-ramps, sidestreets and boulevards, a respectful silence between them as they drive the certain route home.

Over the PA, a woman's voice announces that the department store is now closed, and Phillip sees that his eyes have gotten no further than the end of the building, where an empty counter sits waiting in fluorescence. This is in Lost and Found.

What do you do, Phillip wonders as Rebecca's shadowed face draws closer, what do you do if you're neither?

RUSSELL'S HONOR

Somewhere in Month Nine, I decided to commute my own sentence, throw in the towel, so to speak, as I had on most things in my life – certainly on all things legitimate. It was only later that I remembered Mother's birthday, and only then after being reminded, though I'm sure this fact loomed large in the secret part of my deliberation.

LaPlante was holding up the line that morning as usual, squinting down the taped-up handle of his rake the way drunks who like to pretend otherwise assess a pool cue. In all the times I'd seen LaPlante do this, Drano, who was our Minimum Security, never did give LaPlante another rake, and I suspect if he had LaPlante would've found fault with that one too.

You can see how, in real life, this manner of thinking must have got LaPlante into trouble somewhere along the line, though I'm not sure how it translates into mail fraud, for which LaPlante was donating thirteen months of his precious time. My progression, on the other hand, was a much more linear one: I began life as an inveterate liar, and I remain one to this day. The only thing that's changed is the severity of my lies and what happens when I get caught in them. At least I can say I've been forthright with myself in this respect, and to each of my three wives, to whom I admitted early on my tendency to prevaricate, albeit with a smile on my face. Two of the three would swear on a stack of no-limit MasterCards that I've been faithful to them and always will be. The third, Noreen Sanchez, who is known as the Belle of Pensacola in her native state, would at least attest to my knack for being sociable.

It was Noreen who saw to it that I was prosecuted for bigamy, and it was Noreen who told me at the trial that she wasn't doing it out of spite, which of course meant she was, but that she was doing it for my own good, which of course meant she wasn't. Unless you'd call a year's stint at the Honor Ranch therapeutic, in which case I'd like to deal you a few hands of poker.

Normally, I rode out LaPlante's little rituals with the patience of Mount Rushmore, but as I was newly motivated and wanting to patent my latest brainstorm, I yelled at LaPlante to get a move on. LaPlante's lover, Frank James, who was queued up behind Laplante like always and who claimed to be a descendant of the James clan that shot up that bank in Minnesota and later got shot up themselves, whispered something into one of LaPlante's little rodent ears. The next thing LaPlante is holding up his rake and showing it off to the line, as if it were the exact one he would've chosen had Drano given him a choice.

When I got up to the booth, Drano handed me

rake 417 and wrote the number down in his log. He got a look of real accomplishment on his broad, flat face whenever he performed his duty, and it made you forget for a second that he was quite an ugly man, even in his starched uniform. I wondered sometimes what a person like Drano did in his spare time, when no one was telling him what to do, though I never did wonder enough to ask him. He was a bachelor, I knew that much, and I think it tickled him that I had three wives when he had none and would probably never find anybody, which isn't necessarily a sad thing. A part of me has always admired the Dranos of the world, guys who fell into a hole early in life and weren't smart enough to climb back out or even to know they were in a hole to begin with. It saved you from being stupid in the long run, as I inevitably was, and as long as you had a little luck – didn't find yourself in the infantry or working in a coal shaft – your life would play out just fine, minus all the nasty complications.

'So how's the wife and kids, Bert?' I asked Drano and stared down at the rusted tines of my rake. No one ever called him Drano to his face. It would've been like addressing LaPlante as Fudgeweenie.

There was a little pause while Drano thought up his response. 'My wife cheats on me and my kids beat off,' he said finally. 'You single guys have all the cards.' He tried to hold back a smile, but it started busting out at the seam of his pursed lips, and then his mouth took on the shape of a mallard's.

'Yeah, but I've been out of circulation lately,' I told him and leaned forward against the counter. 'I was thinking I'd put myself back in the rotation today.' I said this last part like it was something confidential, something you'd share with your best bud over a draft. The only thing a habitual liar lacks is credibility, and sometimes spinning the truth works better than spinning what isn't.

'Oh yeah?' Drano said, grinning freely now. 'What time are you going over? The boys and me will give you a twenty-one gunner.' He rubbed his hand across the rosewood butt of his service revolver in the holster by his hip. The *Honor Ranch Gazette* was always making a big deal out of what a great marksman Drano was (District champ three years running), though secretly I wondered if Drano could hit the floor if he fell off a barstool. Still, they could've put someone else in charge of work detail besides Drano, and that gave the story more than enough credence, as far as I was concerned. The state-appointeds, through no ingenuity of their own, were always keeping us guessing.

'I'll give you the high sign when I'm ready,' I told Drano. 'No fireworks till then. OK?'

'You got it, chief,' he said and winked at me with both his eyes.

I hoboed my rake down to the stone field where the rest of the club was waiting. The April sun had cast long shadows out from their bodies, and it made them seem erected there, like the statues on Easter Island. Our job was to gather rocks and put them in the old swimming pool left over from the days when the Honor Ranch was still a dude ranch, when a fellow paid good money to stay there and didn't want to leave. There isn't much rainfall in that part of Oregon, a fact that had come as a revelation to me when I first arrived there. I'd always thought the whole state was like Portland – where I was ultimately arrested – rainy and green and full of bars. The only vegetation at the Honor Ranch is rocks, plus the occasional Doug fir growing along the banks of the Columbia River, which borders the Ranch to the north. The rocks were part of a master plan to build more dormitories, as the warden called them, which is really fancy talk for jails. In my time there, though, I never did see any buildings under construction, and neither had any of the long-termers I surveyed. If they'd told us we were digging our own graves, we would've been more motivated.

We loitered in our shadows for a good fifteen minutes while Drano laid two rakes end to end on the dirt and etched out a circle around them with a third. Then he perched himself on his camp stool in the middle of the circle and blew his whistle, which was the signal for us to start raking. I asked Drano once why he always painted himself into a circle, and he said it was because he didn't want anyone taking a swing at him with a rake. I guess he never thought that somebody could just throw one at him, or cross the line behind him and whack him over the head. In any event, Drano's plan never failed him, though not for any of his convoluted reasons. In truth, violence wasn't necessary to break out of the Honor Ranch, if only because it didn't make sense to break out period, at least from their point of view. The honeymoon suite at the state penitentiary was waiting for you when they reeled you back in, and they figured we were smart enough not to want that. And they were right – I didn't relish a compulsory change in my sexual preference – but the way I saw it, there was no point in waiting when the outcome would be the same regardless. I might as well get on to whatever havoc I had left in me to wreak.

I took up labor next to my dormmate, a computer thief named Vernon Lee, who was raking by himself near the river. Rocks could easily be found there, and you didn't have to waste a lot of time separating them from dirt, assuming you wanted to be industrious. Vernon, for reasons only God could come up with, wanted to be industrious. In 1985, he'd successfully transferred 600K into a Swiss bank account, and the next day had tapped into the police computer in Eugene to tell them what he'd done and where they could pick him up – at a tattoo parlor in Klamath Falls. I have never understood the breed of criminal who confesses, at least when he's not plea bargaining or caught red-handed, and in this regard Vernon had piqued my curiosity. He was a quiet man who studied the Bible in his free time, though he never preached a word at me, which I was grateful for. In my opinion, Vernon was born with too much intellect but with the normal amount of temptations – a deadlier mix than nitro and glycerin.

'Vernon,' I said and listened to my voice trail off over the water, 'what time you got?'

'Two weeks, two days,' he said automatically. He didn't look up, just kept banging away at a chunk of red adobe that he knew Drano wouldn't qualify as

136

stone. Vernon's stint at the Honor Ranch was nearly over, as the bank that had originally pressed charges had also paid for his appeal. They wanted to hire him back as chief of security because someone not as repentant as Vernon was sampling their till. It made me think there was no way Noreen would ever hire *me* back, and even if she wanted to I'd blown all her appeal money buying Lotto tickets and betting the Exacta.

'My watch says forty-five,' I told Vernon and skimmed an agate three times on the Columbia River. 'Minutes, that is.'

He kept on raking like he hadn't heard me. He mashed the adobe he was working on back into the ground with his foot. Then he dug it back out again. 'What time does *their* watch say?' he asked me. He wasn't sure yet if I was straighting him.

'Two moons,' I said.

He picked up the piece of adobe on his rake and tried to heave it into the river, but it fell off as he entered his pitching motion. He was watching me out of the corner of his eye.

'You never did figure out how to synchronize your watch, did you?' he said. This came out of his mouth sadly, the way all things he considered great truths came out of his mouth. He was on the verge of his first sermon, I could see that, so I gave him the face I always gave the state-appointeds whenever they tried to explain right from wrong. The face of an autistic child.

'You know what a random number generator is?' Vernon asked me, but didn't wait for my answer. 'You have one of those for a brain.' He was looking at the place where I was standing, only without looking at me. 'I had this tattoo put on the day I turned myself in,' he said and extended his left hand for my perusal. I'd never gotten a good look at his tattoo until then – it was stitched into his palm – the picture of a cow standing in a pasture.

'I made it six years through the Navy,' he continued, 'and I swore I'd never have one put on. Haven't you ever wondered why somebody does that to themselves? Why they'll tattoo some woman's name on their chest when they know she'll disappear a lot sooner than it will? Did you think it was because they were stupid or macho or not liking themselves very much?'

The fact is I'd never given any thought to why people got tattoos, the same way I'd never thought about why people went bowling or shopping at the mall. Vernon seemed to want an answer this time, though, so I tried to think up something philosophical.

'Maybe they were in love,' I said.

'You could say that,' Vernon said. 'You could say that. They were in love with how they felt, might be a better way of putting it. They knew they felt different at that moment than they ever had in their lives and they wanted to preserve that feeling forever. They wanted to preserve it so when things got bad again they could look back via their tattoo and say, "I remember when that happened. I really felt *good* that day." '

Vernon was smiling now like Buddha himself, only without the pot belly. I still wasn't sure what all this had to do with the cow chewing cud on his left hand, but I suspected his monologue was like most

138

speeches – it needed to be said more than heard.

I grinned back at Vernon as though I'd gained a keen insight into the ways of the universe.

'With the Lord's help I'll live that moment the rest of my life,' he told me. He still had on a smile, though I could see it wasn't attached to his thinking anymore. 'You'll understand if I resume my raking at another part of the river,' he said. 'I've pledged God I'll no longer bear accomplice to sin. That includes others' as well as my own.'

Then he picked up his rake and strode downriver, the sun shining on his back, and on all of our backs, really, though I'm sure Vernon was the only one who gave it any significance. Up the bank, Drano was sitting motionless on his camp stool and looking in another direction, which I took to be a good sign. He was a pacer when things didn't sit right with him, and I was anxious for things to sit right with him that morning.

So I started raking. Raking and thinking, plus my usual amount of dawdling, for appearance's sake, so Drano wouldn't sniff me out. It had always seemed funny to me that they put you to work when you got to the Honor Ranch, since in one way or another we were all there because we'd avoided work in the first place. They should've realized that when a person's forced to rake stones for five hours at a pop the only thing he thinks about is ways to get out of doing it. So, by the time he's served his sentence, the muscle in his brain that cooks up schemes is all built up and callused and ready to work on reflex. If you ask me, they should've issued us chaise longues and umbrella drinks and told us to reflect on our navels.

That way, when we got let out, we'd only be a drain on society, instead of actively putting it in shambles.

In an hour or so, LaPlante walked up to Drano, with Frank James tagging along behind, and I knew this to be my opportunity. I aligned myself with Drano's eyes and the back of LaPlante's bald head and waded out to where the current started, letting it float me downriver. I was never much of a swimmer, but the Columbia didn't seem too deep or wide at that particular bend, and I knew the rapids didn't start for another ten miles west in The Dalles.

At the point of no return I looked back and I suddenly felt how cold the water was, which was the closest I came to regret. I could see Drano, without a clue, still jawing at LaPlante, in all probability over his rake. And I could see Vernon, head down, stacking rocks like there was no tomorrow or even the day after. And I could see the rest of them, too, faking their way through Limbo as I had been for the last nine months, waiting for another chance at Hell. It made me wonder if I would recognize myself from that distance, if I would stick out in some way from your ordinary grafter, but I decided, as I fought off a chill, that I wouldn't, and felt relieved and melancholy all at once.

I knew my baby sister, Angie, had married a man named Drinkwater, and that they'd set up house in a suburb near Portland, but that was all I knew and what I knew was at least ten years old – I hadn't seen or heard of her in that long. The page for Drinkwater had been torn out of the directory, so I tried 411 with all the usual names – John, William, Robert – and a few longshots too – a Clarence and a Horace – but none of these Drinkwaters knew an Angie or at least was willing to own up to it. I was out of change from dialing Information, which was still free on the day I was convicted, so in desperation I opened up the directory to Angela Davis, my sister's maiden name. I was shocked when I found it listed that way, because Angie had always been the straight arrow in our family, and it had embarrassed her no end that her namesake preached communism at the University of California. I dialed Angie collect, not expecting her to accept the charges, and she didn't. I was able to identify her voice, however, which was all I needed since I had her address right in front of me.

By the time I got to Angie's neighborhood, it was getting dark. I'd convinced an old woman behind the counter at the St Vincent de Paul's in Boardman that my seaplane had capsized and she'd given me ten dollars and a suit of dry clothes, including a wide synthetic tie, in exchange for my prison jump suit. I was gambling that her myopic eyes wouldn't decipher the Honor Ranch logo stamped above the breast pocket, and I thought even if she did uncover my real predicament she probably wouldn't turn me in.

Angie's place was a tract house at the end of a cul-de-sac with little palm trees in the front yard and a green spot that shone up at them, even in the twilight. I figured she hadn't done particularly well in the settlement, because from what I remembered Drinkwater was pulling in six figures as an oral

141

surgeon. The house badly needed to be restuccoed and there was a beat-up Nova parked in the driveway with a bumper sticker whose message had long since faded. I pushed the lighted doorbell several times and stood back from the threshold. The last time I'd seen Angie, I'd borrowed her Kharman Ghia for a job interview and wound up in a Mexican jail. They never did release her car, as far as I know.

A little tow-headed girl wearing a party hat and a Bopeep dress answered the door. She didn't look much like Angie, and I couldn't remember enough of Drinkwater's looks to see if there was any resemblance there. She had one of those paper dragon tongues clutched in her hand, the kind you unfurl with your mouth, only it looked like she'd gnawed the end of it clean off.

'Are you a salesman?' she asked me, without being shy.

'No, I'm not,' I told her. 'I'm a consumer from way back.' I don't think she knew what a consumer was, or more probably didn't know the word, because she just stared up at me and began hoisting herself on the doorknob. 'Is your mother in?' I asked her.

'That's what salesmen always say.' She stared at me another beat, then ran back into the house, I hoped to fetch her mother. A cold front was beginning to set in and I didn't have a jacket, and I thought if I could just get half a chance I'd be able to talk my way inside, even if I had picked the wrong house.

In a minute or so the little girl returned with Angie, an Angie with a lot more makeup and blond

142

hair than I remembered. She had on what looked like a dental assistant's uniform, though it could have been a nurse's, and I checked to see if there was a name tag on it. There wasn't. Angie stared at me the way the little girl had, and for a second I could see some resemblance. Then her face clouded and she looked scared and she shepherded the little girl back inside, without ever saying a word.

I stood in the doorway a long while unsure of my next move. Angie hadn't slammed the door in my face, after all, and if she was dialing the police, I figured I'd walk in there and get it from the horse's mouth, instead of waiting for Miranda on the front porch. The only sound from inside was somebody mumbling, or it might've been the TV. It was difficult to hear because the airport was close by and there were planes circling above like buzzards, waiting for their chance to land.

I walked quietly into a white corridor with some baby pictures hung on the paneling and entered the first room on my right. It was small and carpetless, empty except for a stuffed animal whose species I was unable to determine, and a pint-sized bed that I took to be the little girl's. I could hear the mumbling again, only it wasn't mumbling – it was singing without much tune – and it was coming from the end of the hall. I walked heavily this time, so as not to surprise anyone, and entered the kitchen with a smile on my face. I wanted to cast the best light on things in the event I was on my way back to jail.

Around a Formica table sat the little girl and an unkempt old woman whom I pegged as the little girl's sitter. She was wearing dark glasses and had an exaggerated smile painted on her face, which at first made me think she was blind. But then I decided the shades were all wrong – the sort of thing respectable housewives wore in the sixties, but only Elton John would be caught dead wearing now. There was a pineapple upside-down cake on the table and someone had poked birthday candles through the holes in each of the six pineapple slices. The candles weren't lit. Then the little girl saw me and began waving. The old woman shortly followed suit.

'You were always so popular,' Angie said, and I could tell she'd had a few drinks. She was standing behind the table against the refrigerator while she filled the cylinder of a twenty-two with bullets. I almost reminded her that I wasn't Rasputin – it only took one shot to stop me – but I decided sarcasm isn't the best strategy when someone's loading a gun.

'You look good, Angie,' I said.

She closed the twenty-two and regarded it blankly, then regarded me the same way. 'I know that, Russ,' she said and got the kind of sneer on her face I imagined myself having whenever I fantasized about using a gun.

It was clear she still harbored a lot of resentment toward me and I couldn't say I blamed her. I hadn't set out to steal her car ten years before, but I'm sure at some point I got one of my bright ideas, and after that one thing had turned bad after another. It seemed to me that Angie's life hadn't turned out as she'd intended it either, though I couldn't say I had ever really intended mine. At that moment she could lay the blame on somebody else for her problems –

144

namely me – and it was making her feel a whole lot better about things.

'You really do look good, Russ,' Angie said and laughed, though not because anything was funny. 'You ought to have yourself filmed while you shirk responsibility. You'd sell more of them than Jane Fonda's sold workout tapes.'

'He's not a salesman,' the little girl said and began swinging her legs under the table. The old woman waved at me again.

'Is it all right if I sit down?' I asked Angie. 'It's been a long day.'

'Sure,' she said, 'right there on the floor. I know it must be hard work breaking out of jail.'

The way she said it, I couldn't tell if she was being serious or not. I wouldn't have put it past Noreen to call up every one of my living relatives and tell them what I'd done, though I doubted she could've found Angie.

Out of the blue, the old woman started singing 'Happy Birthday' to herself, and I realized it was her I'd eavesdropped in the hall. She got as far as the second line and then started again: 'Happy birthday to me, Happy birthday to me,' and she sang it that way over and over while the little girl giggled and banged the table with a fork. The mean-spirited smile on Angie's face had faded and now she looked like she wanted to cry but had lost the ability to do so. I thought for a second she might fire a warning shot over our heads, like the police always did on TV when they wanted a suspect to halt. But then just as quickly the old woman ceased her wailing, and Angie grasped the fork out of the

145

little girl's hand and carefully laid it on the table.

'When do we get cake?' the little girl asked, and I wasn't sure if she was asking me or Angie.

'In a little while, honey,' Angie said, 'after Mommy takes care of some business.'

I didn't like the way she said 'business' – it was a euphemism for too many horrible things. I had used that word many a time myself just before the roof came tumbling down, and not on top of me.

'So there must be a motive for your little visit,' Angie said. 'Or were you just stopping in to say Happy Birthday?' She'd regained her nasty tone and then some.

'I was in the neighborhood,' I said.

'What's the matter? Didn't anyone leave their keys in the ignition?'

'I wanted to see how you were doing,' I said, which was at least partly true. I mostly wanted to find a place for the night since I was out of money and didn't think the police would find me there. They'd check the hostels and the Salvation Army and probably wouldn't go any further.

'Oh, we're just tip-top,' Angie said. 'Opportunity is knocking all over the place, can't you tell?' She gestured around the room with her gun. 'I look into people's mouths all day, and when I find something wrong I tell the doctor and he fixes everything. The world is full of doctors, spreading cheer and happiness all over the place. It's hard not to be elated all the time – when you're part of such a great conspiracy, I mean – but I've learned to keep it pretty much under control.'

'At least you have your health,' I told her. 'And a

146

beautiful daughter.' I winked at the little girl and she smiled back at me.

Angie's mouth hardened. 'I don't want you including Jenny in any of this,' she said. 'Hers is the only life I won't allow you to taint around here. The rest of us, it doesn't really matter. We've been painless for years now.'

She looked sadly down at the old woman and touched the top of her gray matted hair. The old woman seemed to take it as a hostile gesture, though, and began slapping furiously at Angie's hand, which she withdrew and breathed on as though it needed warming.

'She's sixty years old today,' Angie said, 'and she's crazy as the day she left us.'

It took me a second to realize that Angie had meant me as part of that 'us' and not her little girl. The old woman in the sunglasses and the pasted-up grin was our mother, and it struck me as only fitting that she would reappear the same way she'd disappeared all those years ago, with it happening right before my eyes and me not even noticing. I tried to remember something quiet about her or plain, but I could only recall the lunacy and the long weeks after when my father would return home from his searching, drunk and without any clues. Now she was just another baglady to me. The events in my life had caused me to forget her long ago, to forget what it's like to have a mother or even what it's like to miss one. I had no curiosity as to how Angie had located her, when my father had failed at it so miserably. It was history that made no impact on me; I wanted my life to move forward and I didn't care how it got there.

147

Angie's free hand was balled up against her mouth as if she were trying to keep from spoiling a joke. 'You didn't recognize your own mother, did you, Russell?' She was in a state of amazement. 'Do you recognize yourself when you look in the mirror or do you have to poke yourself to make sure it's you?'

'I don't believe in mirrors,' I told her.

'Do you believe in fate, Russell? Do you believe in karma?' She turned to the little girl. 'I want you to go into the living room and watch TV, now, sweetheart.'

'What about cake?' the little girl asked.

'Mommy will bring you cake when she's done with her business, darling. You just run along now.'

The little girl poked the old woman in the ribs and ran past me to the living room before she could be slapped. I heard the TV go on while Angie stared at me in a way she'd never stared at me before, and I could hear the sound of cars piling up against one another on the TV and the little girl giggling. Angie moved toward me with both her hands on the gun, and when she was within two feet of me she stopped and pointed it right at my face. 'Roll over on your stomach and put your arms behind your back, please,' she said. I could see she meant business, so I lay down on the linoleum with my chin resting on the carpet in the hall. Then I put my hands, palms up, out over my kidneys and waited for whatever came next.

'Rick insisted that I take all the right defense classes when we were still married,' Angie said. 'We were living in a gated community then, but he thought some drug-crazed freak might break in and try to rob us. Everything can be taken from you, if you let it be taken, Russell. I only figured out later who I should be aiming guns at. I guess if you survive you're bound to learn a few things.'

I heard her move closer and then I didn't hear anything. The old woman started belching. There were explosions on the TV. 'I know things are automatic for you,' Angie said. She was very close to me now. I could smell the gin and perfume. 'Have you ever committed a crime of passion, Russell? Have you ever taken a swing at somebody for the sheer meanness of it? Some of us try to do what's right and others do what's right for them. God doesn't favor either one, Russell – He just watches to see what the outcome is.'

She pushed the nozzle of the gun up against the base of my head and I closed my eyes. I tried to connect up what had led to where but I lost track like always. My death would yield up no more clues than anything else had. There would be no aggregation of events, no summary, no life flashing before my eyes, no benevolence or hatred. Just the sound of my own breath being muffled in a carpet and the music from a commercial playing in another room. I tried to lift myself up but couldn't; the gun kept me suspended there, like a butterfly stuck on a pin. Then I said something without thinking, without calculating even its general effect.

'I want to feel bad,' I told her.

And if I'm dead now while I'm telling you all this, then the transition from life was incredibly smooth. Angie took the gun away and started to cry, and when I opened up my eyes again I saw the little girl's little saddle shoes with her little feet stuck in them. 'When do we get cake?' she asked and this time Angie served it up, to all of us, and we sang 'Happy Birthday' clear through to the end. Sometimes when I tell the story we have ice cream with our cake too, though it's always Jenny's birthday and never the old woman's. If somebody asks I say my folks died together in 1965, in a plane crash near Mexico City, that they enjoyed a long and prosperous marriage and had many beautiful grandchildren. I was the only one who went wrong, I explain, and that was years after they had passed away.

I always conclude by showing off my tattoo. It's carved into the palm of my left hand, just like Vernon Lee's, only it's the picture of a pineapple and nothing more. And yes, I tell them, even if they don't ask, it hurt like hell to have it put on, hurts me now just to think about it. Thank God for little favors.

A MINOR FOREST

Kleinbaum's only legacy was a cat, nameless and huge, that lay grunting in its sleep on Langer's small, white stomach. The cat had always made noises while it slept, even when Kleinbaum was still alive, but now that it had invaded Langer's space, a new assortment of bleatings and snarls had started emanating from it, noises that spooked Langer sometimes late at night, spooked him now as he stared at it in the gray noon, with snow, the first of the season, dropping carefully outside. Langer had told everyone in the house about the cat's weirdness, but *their* rooms all had doors, which they could and did shut at night, and the idea of being haunted by Kleinbaum's cat merely seemed amusing to them.

Langer was the only one left in the house without a regular job now, and lately he had begun to think the rest resented him for it, or worse, felt somehow above him. They had voted back in October, for instance, with Langer abstaining, that Langer should be the one to feed the cat, since he'd brought Kleinbaum into the house to begin with. Unfortunately, this left Langer wide open for the cat's vague inclinations: it went about life the way

Kleinbaum had, with little clumps of movement here and there and long periods of contemplation in between.

Sometimes the cat would disappear for hours, and even days, at a time, when Langer could hear it dragging itself around in the attic, and then emerge again according to some nocturnal signal that only wild animals and small children are able to detect. The cat was forever hoisting itself onto the sofa bed in the parlor, where Langer spent his nights, and before long Langer's dreams would ferment, resolving themselves in ways that were at once simple and violent. On several occasions he had tried putting the cat outside, but each time it had made such a fuss, moaning and scratching at the window, that he had reluctantly let it back in.

And the thing was, he hadn't even liked Kleinbaum. Kleinbaum was seriously into his own brain. He was a brainfucker, was what he was, though Kleinbaum had always called himself a poet. This was Grade A pharmaceutical bullshit in Langer's opinion – Kleinbaum was no more a poet than any of the roommates they'd gotten from the Ad Board at the Co-op, and the only reason he'd suggested Kleinbaum in the first place was because Kleinbaum was from the burbs down south, like he was, and had a cash deposit that he could use as float money without anyone else knowing. Kleinbaum hadn't mentioned anything about a cat when he signed the lease. He'd just shown up with it a week later – with the cat and a cardboard box filled with books on philosophy, including a Bible. Langer had sold the books for the paltry sum of sixteen dollars after Kleinbaum's death, but he'd kept the Bible because the man at the bookstore had offered him only two dollars for it, and it came with a special waterproof container that Kleinbaum said would float away at the time when everything else was sinking. This was all Kleinbaum had ever said about the Bible, though it always seemed to be lying open on his nightstand whenever Langer had gone through his belongings.

Everything about Kleinbaum was a mystery to Langer, who was teaching himself to be a drummer. He wasn't into words the way Kleinbaum was. Words could only gum up your thinking, they couldn't make it any clearer. The cat made a noise like a crow, and Langer, unraveled, sat up on his elbows, readying himself for whatever came next. When the cat made the noise again, Langer unraveled even more. He lay back down and made an effort to trance himself, from the cat and all the TV that was happening in his life, the way Blackwell himself did whenever *he* stretched out, with his eyes thrown back in his head like someone in an epileptic seizure.

Langer had seen Blackwell play all night once at the Ear Club in Portland, and afterward Langer told Kleinbaum that he, Langer, wasn't the same anymore, that he wouldn't be able to stop himself until he could do Blackwell, could *be* Blackwell, at least for one jam. Kleinbaum had looked at him with his single expression, which was really no expression at all. 'How will you know it when it happens?' he asked. This was just vintage Kleinbaum as far as Langer was concerned. You couldn't say anything to Kleinbaum without him saying some smartass thing. You couldn't fucking breathe while he was around, he'd fucking analyze your lungs. Just mute, Langer used to tell him. And Kleinbaum would respond, 'Words are a commercial for the soul.' It was no wonder Kleinbaum had offed himself, Langer thought. He didn't want to give anyone the satisfaction of murdering him first.

The cat snorted and Langer, only half-hypnotized, threw the blankets and the cat along with them onto the hardwood floor. He ran his eyes down his skinny white body, all the way to his skinny white toes. He wiggled them but didn't smile. Then he noticed a purple crescent-shaped mark on his left hand. It was the distinguishing symptom of some new and ill-defined plague, he decided, incurable but not fatal, the kind of disease that kept you just alive enough to suffer. He picked up one of his sticks, which were wedged in the machinery of the sofa bed, and pressed it hard against the center of the mark, then lifted it up again and watched the blood run back into the depression.

In a few weeks he wouldn't see what he was seeing. There wasn't any cause and effect when you were in pain, just the effect. And there wasn't any time either. You just lay there helpless, stuck in this one God-awful moment. Pain was the opposite of infinity, Langer decided and became angry when he realized he was beginning to sound like Kleinbaum. He played a little seven-four on the back of his hand until it hurt. Then he remembered that the mark had been stamped on by the doorman at Rosie's where he'd gigged the night before for beers –

he was still routinely carded though he had recently turned thirty. He relaxed and shut his eyes, letting his arm dangle off the side of the bed.

Then he felt how cold he was.

He looked over at the cat. It was in the same place he'd thrown it, still under the covers, sitting like a colossal lump of gravy waiting to be stirred. He put his fingers in his ears, but he could still hear the sound, even above the monotonous rhythm of his heart: Kleinbaum's cat was purring.

It's all TV, Langer reminded himself. The thing with TV, the thing that made TV something you could deal with, was that it had a plug. Down in LA, TV could be a problem. There was so much of it there you could spend your whole life unplugging it, assuming you could find all the outlets, which was no day at the beach. Up here there were trees. Up here you could stand outside in the trees and the quiet they generated would shut you right down.

Trees, Langer told himself, and lifted himself up off the sofa.

He walked naked to the bay window and put his eye up to the bullet hole, staring out into the street. He felt vulnerable for a second and then remembered that the rest of the window was frosted. He could see a clump of apple trees nested in some snow and beyond the orchard more trees, pine and fir and cottonwood trees, fanned out in all directions. Birch's Doberman was in the foreground, peeing on the post of the YIELD sign at the corner. Langer looked over at Birch's house, where two pine trees on either side of it were preventing snow from falling on the roof.

Birch's mother had already left for work, or at least her Mercury was gone. The place was quiet. This made Langer more nervous than if he'd seen Birch in the front yard firing his M16 at mockingbirds. Birch was one sick puppy in Langer's estimation. He was a long-hair now, whereas in the sixties, if he'd been anything but a wham-bam waiting to happen, he'd have had a flat top, kicking hippie ass and taking names later. Langer wore his hair short, but he'd been a freak in 1969 at the age of thirteen. His father had handcuffed him one day to the hose reel in the backyard and cut off his hair with a pair of garden shears. This had been the first of a long line of troubles between Langer and his father, who had died last year of stomach cancer.

He thought about his eye framed perfectly in the bullet hole and imagined a second bullet fired from the same location lodging itself into his pupil. Like Robin Hood, he thought, splitting arrow with arrow. He stepped away from the window and said 'TV' out loud, listening to his voice rattle in the wall furnace. It sounded like a furnace all right. And what he was standing on felt like a floor. He moved back to the window, thinking 'window', and let his finger run slowly down the glass.

The garage door on the house next to Birch's was mechanically opening, and when it had locked in place, out stepped King White Daddy in the shroud of his own breath. Everyone in the house called him King White Daddy, except for Kleinbaum, who had called him by his real name, Mr Stewart. He was moving in Langer's direction, in a bright orange bathrobe and cowboy boots that came up to the bases of his pudgy white knees, and Langer could see, even at this distance, the look of real determination on his jowly face, that weird determination that he used to detail his van and tempt girls Birch's age to go for rides.

He was freak all right, Langer thought, like Birch, only he'd been around so long his kinks were part of the system. None of *his* crimes were on the books, the way Langer's were. There was a warrant out for Langer's arrest, for example, for a dine-and-dash at the Bob's in Thousand Oaks. And Langer was currently dealing mushrooms, which he grew under the house, the kind of mushrooms that opened up your space suit and poured the universe right in. The plan was to keep selling until he could gig for regular pay, but recently his business had begun to tail off. The trend was toward the harder edges of speed and coke now, or quitting altogether and moving back to LA to get a full-time job. Even Langer's regulars, freak's freaks, Langer called them, were moving north again, as they'd moved north from San Francisco in the seventies. Langer saw himself by 2000 with the rest of his dwindled stock, basking in the midnight sun along the Bering Strait.

He stepped away from the window and slipped on his kimono, which was wadded up in the back of his bass drum. He could hear King White Daddy coming up the steps and he considered whether he should answer the door. At first he didn't, though not because he'd made any decision not to. When King White Daddy knocked again, Langer again kept quiet. Then Kleinbaum's cat, having unveiled itself, moved between Langer's ankles and began scratching at the base of the door.

'You fuckers,' Langer said under his breath, meaning King White Daddy and the cat, who always had to pee at the wrong times. Langer was categorically against litter boxes, especially since his mother worked for a company that made them, along with every other useless household accessory. The cat stopped scratching and looked up at Langer, with its stupid little Kleinbaum expression, Langer thought. It never made any noise when it was supposed to.

He opened the door a crack and peered out at King White Daddy, who was studying some bullet holes on the side of the house. The bullets seemed to form a question mark, as though they'd been fired deliberately in this pattern. The cat forced the door open with its head, but when it saw the tips of King White Daddy's boots, it backed up into the house and ran to the furnace, where it quickly returned to character. Langer stared out at King White Daddy's face. It looked the same as it had when it was still across the street. Only now it was much bigger.

A voice came up out of King White Daddy then, like the spume out of a whale: 'You going to let me in, Space? Or are we going to do this thing by séance?'

That's what King White Daddy always called him, Space. Langer didn't have an opinion on it one way or another.

'What thing are we doing?' Langer asked.

When King White Daddy didn't respond, Langer opened the door wide. He was still looking at the bullet holes. 'Something's been tearing up your siding,' he said. 'You got woodpeckers, Space?' He turned and faced Langer and stamped his boots on an empty catfood bag that Langer had set out for a doormat. 'Looks like this house is made out of peckerwood to me.'

Langer shrugged and moved silently back into the kitchen. When he came back with his water pipe, King White Daddy was standing inside with his eye up to the bullet hole in the window. Langer lit his pipe. TV was a lot funnier when you were stoned, Langer thought.

'I guess you got glass peckers, too,' King White Daddy said.

'We've got all kinds of peckers,' Langer said. 'They'll peck just about anything you can think of.'

In truth, Birch had shot up the house the day before with his rifle. This was because Birch was a mean fucker and didn't like the way Langer played his drums. The same kind of shit happened in the burbs, Langer thought, only down there nothing was ever allowed to get weird out in the open. Instead it festered and turned back on itself and pretty soon you'd die on the inside with a hard little smile on your face. That's what had happened to King White Daddy. You could blow him to Kingdom Come and that twisted little grin of his would fall back to earth in one piece.

Langer looked at the back of King White Daddy's bald pink head and smirked. The pipe was filling up the room with the sweet smell of marijuana. He took in a deep drag and held it.

'A little early in the day, isn't it?' King White Daddy said. He was still squinting through the bullet hole.

Langer exhaled, deliberately in the cat's direction. 'The whole day might as well be early,' he said. 'Better early than never.' He had played this game with King White Daddy before and this time he didn't plan on losing. King White Daddy would have to say what he wanted. Langer wasn't about to ask him for it.

'I heard about your bro, man,' King White Daddy said, and looked over at Kleinbaum's cat. 'What he want to go and do a funny thing like that for?'

Langer tried to think up something clever, but his brain cramped up and he couldn't think of anything. It made him angry that King White Daddy could get under his skin. 'I told him he couldn't blow his brains out in the house,' he blurted finally, not liking the sound of his own voice. It was as though he were listening to himself on a tape recorder. 'I found his gun in a Ziploc bag under the sink. I don't like cleaning up other people's messes.'

He could still remember the look of routine disappointment on Kleinbaum's face when he told him this, the way a child looks when he's asked to play outside. Still, he was shocked when Kleinbaum actually killed himself – up against the recycling bin in the Safeway parking lot downtown. The bullet had gone in through his left eye and come out the back of his skull, tearing a large hole in it, but you could still see his mouth perfectly – it was formed into a little half smile, like the expression on a gingerbread boy. Kleinbaum's mother had never come to

160

claim his body and eventually Langer was asked to make the ID. He hadn't flinched when they pulled Kleinbaum out in a drawer, though he had stayed up all night wondering about the guy who'd cleaned up the mess in the parking lot. He decided it was the kind of job he was given whenever he synched with the TV world. Only they'd never show that job on TV, just the smartass detective putting the pieces together with the masking-tape outline of Kleinbaum's body in the background.

Langer caught himself staring at King White Daddy, who was now staring back. He lifted the pipe to his lips and took a long drag without averting his gaze.

King White Daddy smiled. His eyes were the color of lead. 'Well, I guess that makes him some kind of martyr then.'

Langer answered without letting go of the smoke. 'He didn't have a cause. You have to have a cause for that.'

'You shouldn't talk with your mouth full.'

Langer let the smoke out in a gust. 'I asked him why and he told me he just wanted to get it over with.'

'Maybe he's the Saint of No Reason,' King White Daddy said. He was doing his smiling bit again. 'I can't think of a better thing to die for.' He stepped away from the window toward Kleinbaum's cat, though carefully, as if it might spring up at him. 'Still, that's a funny place to park your soul.'

He lifted a foot above the cat's head, but the cat just sat there, not caring if King White Daddy was mean enough to step on it, or even knowing he was about to. Kleinbaum had raised the cat on brewer's yeast to accelerate its growth, and now everything about it was swelled, including its brain.

King White Daddy brought his foot down as hard as he could, missing the cat's head by a fraction of an inch. Langer heard the loud smack a short time after, as though he were watching from some great distance. The cat rolled over with its legs in the air, its stomach exposed for petting.

'Cat's been smoking the same shit you have,' King White Daddy said.

Langer pointed his hand at King White Daddy's torso and clicked an imaginary button. He wondered what Kleinbaum would have done in this situation, and decided not anything.

'At least you've got opposable thumbs,' King White Daddy said. 'You just might work out after all.'

'Jesus,' Langer said and laughed. 'This must be cable. They don't show anything like this on the networks.'

'Depends on what network you're referring to.'

'It doesn't depend on anything,' Langer said angrily and got mad at himself for being mad. 'I don't know what the fuck we're talking about.'

'Opposable thumbs,' King White Daddy said as though this were abundantly clear. 'What separates our kind from the rest of Noah's party. Sometimes, in this world of consumerism and government outlays, a person loses track of the fundamentals. Forgets his hands can actually pick something off a tree and put it in his own mouth.' His smile seemed to snap into place. 'As opposed to endorsing food stamps at your local Safeway. Follow me?'

Langer nodded anyway.

'Our Uncle Sam just wrote me a long letter. The bottom line says opposable thumbs – with your standard "Sincerely", of course. Naturally, since we're in the middle of the holiday season, I thought of trees.'

He stared at Langer as though they'd rehearsed this conversation and it was Langer's turn to speak.

'Trees,' Langer repeated.

'In LA, those aluminum jobs are out of favor. They want the real thing now. It's their one shot during the year to redeem themselves, and even though they know it won't work, they're willing to give it a shot. A tree might give them fifteen or twenty minutes of satisfaction. That's a lot more than they get out of sex.'

Langer could feel himself being sucked right into the screen. Go with it, he told himself. But he didn't feel high enough yet. 'How do you know so much about LA?' he said. 'I doubt you've ever been south of Portland.'

'It's that other network I was telling you about,' King White Daddy said. 'I think you need some new plugs, Space. Your neurons are beginning to misfire.'

'Just say no,' Langer told himself, though aloud, and took another hit. He waited for the smoke to reach his lungs, which were rapidly filling up with cold air.

'You can't draw off a pipe that ain't lit,' King White Daddy said and shook his large bare head. 'You can't cash your welfare if it ain't been mailed.'

He undid the belt on his robe and carefully retied it, as though he were folding an origami. 'I thought I'd get you and Birch out there with a couple of axes and lay waste to a minor forest. Then we'd drive the trees down to LA and collect the reward money. Your cut would buy you a year's supply of your favorite contraband.' He moved closer to Langer and actually touched him on the shoulder. 'You could hibernate eleven months of the year. I wouldn't be back to wake you until the first of next December.'

You can pick up Kleinbaum first, Langer thought, and flashed King White Daddy a dopey grin. He'd beaten the asshole at his own game. 'What do I say?' Langer said. 'What do I fucking have to say about that?'

'Chin music,' King White Daddy said and withdrew his hand. 'Your lips are moving, but your mouth isn't getting anywhere.'

'Birch is a squirrel.'

King White Daddy made a face that was something near earnest. 'He's a big squirrel, though. Lions and tigers and game wardens all roam around out there.' He squatted and stroked Kleinbaum's cat, which was still turned over on its back. 'My motto is, "Speak softly and carry an automatic weapon." '

'Jesus,' Langer said and lit up the pipe again. He imagined his tiny image along with King White Daddy's, broken up by lines, the way the picture looks when you get up too close. You could never turn it off once you were inside, Langer thought. You were part of it then.

He didn't need any Kleinbaum to tell him that.

*   *   *

164

If you'd seen the three of them sitting together on a Ferris wheel, you would have been tempted to call the police, although it would've been difficult to explain what you thought was wrong. In the front seat of a U-Haul truck, however, they looked practically normal, and they passed, without arousing an iota of suspicion, a busload of handicapped children who simpered and waved and a large sheriff in a patrol car transporting a diminutive prisoner.

Langer was sitting in the middle with King White Daddy driving and Birch staring out into the woods while he spit sunflower husks into a Styrofoam cup. Birch's rifle, which was propped up against the glove compartment, had a machine-embroidered strap on it, the kind Langer had seen a few years back on every other folk guitar. He wanted to ask Birch where he'd stashed the guitarist's body, but he thought better of it and stared out the windshield at a thunder-head that seemed to be painted on the sky. He was angry because he was cold and King White Daddy had promised he'd buy them breakfast an hour ago and now they were in the middle of Bumfuck, Egypt, halfway to Tim-fuck-tu, where there weren't any short-order cooks, let alone diners for them to cook in.

The snow was falling freely now, but they were going to the foothills to cut down trees anyway, despite avalanche warnings in the mountains and the threat of black ice. Kleinbaum had always said there were no middles in life, only beginnings and endings, but as far as Langer was concerned, life was all middle, with no idea how you got there and no idea how you got out. He leaned over and fished an apple, his fourth of the morning, out of the day-pack at his feet and started to peel the skin off it as though it were an orange. Birch's Doberman had begun to whimper in the back of the truck, and periodically Birch would slam his fist against the cab wall and the dog would be quiet for another minute or so and then start up again.

'You know what the Bible says about apples,' Birch said and rolled down his window. The truck was passing a field that seemed to be carved out of the woods. He picked up his rifle and began sighting Brahma cows; they were staring listlessly out at the road, as if they'd been waiting too long to be retrieved.

'I didn't know you were so religious,' Langer said and took a large bite of the apple. He wasn't sure what the Bible said about apples, except for the part about Eve, of course, who struck Langer as the only normal one in the whole story. He was tempted to check it out in Kleinbaum's Bible, which was in the daypack beneath him, but he didn't want Birch to know he had it.

'I personally don't have any affiliation with reli-giousness,' Birch said and aimed his rifle at a young cow nuzzling up to its mother. 'Now my old lady, she's a different story. Always telling me what this sign means, or what this man on TV is really trying to tell us. My old lady can read a recipe on the back of a Ritz Cracker box and give you, in hours and seconds, when the locusts will start pouring from the sky.'

Birch stared out the windshield as though he

expected to see locusts swarming on the truck. A flicker of disappointment crossed his face when he saw that there weren't any – the only thing beyond them was the funnel of the road. 'My old lady says when they come they'll be in a big twister,' he said. 'Can you imagine that? A twister made of locusts. You'd be caught up in a whole new web of life, spinning around with a bunch of fucking grasshoppers.' He loaded up his mouth with sunflower seeds and looked out over his rifle. The Doberman was howling again in the back of the truck, but he didn't seem to hear it.

'Naw, you can have your Jesus,' Birch said and fired a shot into the air. The noise was so loud it made Langer feel as if the bullet had come from inside his own head. 'I'll take a nuke shelter and a few cans of Raid any day of the week. Wasn't a man nor bug created couldn't be taken out with the right equipment.'

'Amen,' King White Daddy said.

Langer looked over at him to see if he was serious. He was smiling his usual smile, though, as if his mind could see one frame ahead of everything that happened.

'Like shooting buffalo from a train,' Birch said matter-of-factly and fired a shot at a Brahma bull just before it disappeared from view. Langer watched the bull's knees buckle in the sideview mirror, and then the image was replaced by an endless line of cottonwood trees. It was as though the truck were stationary now and the woods were moving all around them.

'Cows go to cow heaven if they've been good,'

Birch said and winked at King White Daddy. 'People go to cow heaven if they've been bad.'

'Where's that leave Space here?' King White Daddy said.

Langer pushed the cigarette lighter in on the dash-board. He was in dire need of some TV serum, especially since he was getting a stereo broadcast. Then he remembered that he'd left his marijuana on the dining-room table back at the house. His roommates, or even worse, Kleinbaum's cat, had probably devoured it by now.

Will you shut that fucking window, he thought, and then realized he'd said it. There was no turning back. 'It's like fucking Pluto in here.'

'The sensitive artist,' Birch said and tossed the Styrofoam cup out into the snow. 'As long as you're comfy, right? If it's a cold day in Hell, just turn up the thermostat and put on your slippers.' He rubbed his hand down the barrel of his rifle as though he were stroking a cat. 'You just lay back,' he said. 'The rest of us'll fend off the Cubans for you.' He seemed to hear something in what he had just said, as if for once his thoughts and words were connected. It was the first time Langer could remember seeing him smile, and it seemed to fuel something inside him that Langer didn't care to know about.

'What would you fucking do if this was Ground Zero, asswipe?' Birch said. 'Would you roll up all the fucking windows and fire up a doob?' He was glaring at Langer while Langer watched him from the corner of his eye. 'Or maybe you'd just croak yourself like that queerbait Jesus you used to shack up with.'

Langer manufactured a sneer and kept looking out the windshield. 'The Marines only want a few good men,' he said. 'Like you, white boy.'

King White Daddy laughed. 'A white boy calls a white boy white,' he said, and pounded the steering wheel with glee.

The cigarette lighter popped out on the dash and Birch grabbed it with one hand and held Langer's arm with the other. 'This'll warm you up,' Birch said and pushed the lighter hard against the underside of Langer's wrist. With his free hand, Langer gave Birch several quick rabbit punches on the ear until he let go of the lighter, while King White Daddy slapped at them both and told them to fucking simmer down. The truck swerved and King White Daddy steered away from the skid, causing the truck to go into a spin. Langer shut his eyes and could hear Birch's dog slamming against the side of the trailer. He could hear Birch moaning like someone in a nightmare. He could hear King White Daddy silent as he cranked the wheel. And when the truck had turned over and he was lying draped over Birch with his eyes wide open, he could hear the wind outside, blowing on the trees.

He looked up at King White Daddy, who was trying to squirm out of his seat belt in midair, like a crayfish jabbed on a hook. The thought of being sandwiched between King White Daddy and Birch made him panic, and when he had convinced himself that locusts were striking the truck, he kicked violently at a place where the windshield was cracked until there was a hole large enough for him to crawl through. He removed himself completely in a matter of seconds and stood in a bank of snow with little bits of hail falling on his head, watching the truck in a deadpan as he would a TV, even though Birch was probably dead and King White Daddy was probably dying. He realized he was seeing the world through Kleinbaum's eyes for the first time, and it didn't make him mad because Kleinbaum wouldn't be mad, he would just quietly assess the outcome. It didn't have anything to do with thinking you were right. It had to do with processing whatever came next. It didn't have anything to do with anything. It was what happened, not what you thought had happened.

He walked back to the truck and peered inside. King White Daddy was on top of Birch, and Birch's arm was pounding him on the leg as though out of reflex. Langer saw in their faces that they had changed now, too, and he reached inside and took hold of Kleinbaum's Bible, which was still in its waterproof container, then picked up Birch's rifle and dragged it outside by its strap. The Doberman was whimpering in the back of the truck and Langer looked over into the trees seeing green then black and walked around to the rear of the truck and fired several shots into the trailer until all was quiet. He moved to the front of the truck again and kicked out the remaining glass and said, 'Trees,' and without looking behind him backed up until his hand touched wood and he couldn't see into the cab anymore, and fired several shots in that direction and stopped when he was tired and sat against a tree in the middle of trees with Kleinbaum's Bible open to wherever it fell.

We would have you be clear about those who sleep in death, brothers, the Bible said, and he unlaced his left boot and removed it, and removed the sock, and picked up Birch's rifle and put the muzzle in his mouth as far back as it would go, and placed his large toe against the trigger. For if we believe that Jesus died and rose, God will bring forth with him from the dead those who have fallen asleep believing in him. He shut his eyes, wide awake, and opened them again, and when he saw a woman cradling Kleinbaum's cat walking toward him from the road, he went with it, relished it, in fact, because he knew even Kleinbaum hadn't seen this one. This was Kleinbaum's mother.

She was a small woman, dressed simply, in a powder-blue peasant dress that made her skin look like wax, and when it occurred to him that she resembled his own mother, his joy at seeing her quickly faded. He wanted to be angry with her, to blame her, to make her give what she had withheld for all those years. But when she stood above him, looking down, her face as sweet and immutable as a cow's, he saw that she couldn't see his pain, or that she was incapable of feeling it; you could have put a gun to her head and she'd still look out at you with the same clear eyes.

His toe steadily pushed down the trigger until he couldn't think of any reason to stop himself, and then he took the rifle out of his mouth and laid it deliberately on the ground. He felt numb and rolled over on his stomach – the snow was white-hot and burnt him on the cheek.

171

'Are you dead, son?' a familiar voice asked, though the words were as strange as they could be. Langer closed his eyes and thought about it for a moment, and when he turned back over, he saw King White Daddy staring down at him, with Birch, holding his jaw in place, standing right beside him. The trees and everything else were pointing to the sky, which was as unreadable as he remembered it: the clouds were seamless like the snow.

Langer shook his head. 'No,' he told them, and didn't feel the least bit wise. 'I'd know Heaven if I saw it.'

THE END

God Knows
Joseph Heller

'Mr Heller is dancing at the top of his form again . . .
original, sad, wildly funny and filled with roaring'
MORDECAI RICHLER, NEW YORK TIMES BOOK REVIEW

Joseph Heller's powerful, wonderfully funny, deeply
moving novel is the story of David – yes, *that* David:
warrior king of Israel, husband of Bathsheba, father of
Solomon, slayer of Goliath, and psalmist nonpareil . . . as
well as the David we've never known before now: David
the cocky Jewish kid, David the fabulous lover, David the
plagiarised poet, David the Jewish father, David the
(one-time) crony of God . . .

At last, David is telling his own story, and he's holding
nothing back – equally unembarrassed by his faults, his
sins, his prowess, his incomparable glory . . .

God Knows is an ancient story, a modern story, a love
story. It is a novel about growing up and growing old,
about men and women, about fathers and sons, about man
and God. It is a novel of emotional force, imaginative
richness, and unbridled comic invention. It is
quintessential Heller.

'Joseph Heller is the outstandingly clever ideas-man of
modern fiction . . . brilliantly inventive'
JONATHAN RABAN, SUNDAY TIMES

'The unforgiving genius still flares, and the book is worth
the price of admission for the first few pages alone'
MARTIN AMIS, THE OBSERVER

0 552 99169 4

BLACK SWAN

Tales of the City
Armistead Maupin

'Read him'
HARPER'S & QUEEN

A naive young secretary forsakes Cleveland for San
Francisco, tumbling headlong into a brave new world of
laundromat Lotharios, cut throat debutantes, and Jockey
Shorts dance contests. The saga that ensues is manic,
romantic, tawdry, touching, and outrageous –
unmistakably the handiwork of Armistead Maupin.

'Maupin is a richly gifted comic author'
THE OBSERVER

'Like those of Dickens and Wilkie Collins, Armistead
Maupin's novels have all appeared originally as serials
. . . It is the strength of this approach, with its fantastic
adventures and astonishingly contrived coincidences, that
makes these novels charming and compelling'
THE LITERARY REVIEW

'San Francisco is fortunate in having a chronicler as witty
and likeable as Armistead Maupin'
THE INDEPENDENT

0 552 99384 0

BLACK SWAN

The Cider House Rules
John Irving

'Bound to make as vivid an impression as **The World According to Garp**' said *Publishers Weekly* of John Irving's magnificent new novel spanning six decades.

Set among the apple orchards of rural Maine, it is a perverse world in which Homer Wells' odyssey begins. As the oldest unadopted offspring at St Cloud's orphanage, he learns about the skills which, in one way or another, help young and not-so-young women, from Wilbur Larch, the orphanage's founder, a man of rare compassion and with an addiction to ether.

Dr. Larch loves all his orphans, especially Homer Wells. It is Homer's story we follow, from his early apprenticeship in the orphanage surgery, to his adult life running a cider-making factory and his strange relationship with the wife of his closest friend.

'John Irving has been compared with Kurt Vonnegut and J. D. Salinger, but is arguably more inventive than either. Wry, laconic, he sketches his characters with an economy that springs from a feeling for words and mastery over his craft. This superbly original book is one to be read and remembered'
THE TIMES

'The Cider House Rules is difficult to define and impossible not to admire'
DAILY TELEGRAPH

'Like the rest of Irving's fiction, it is often disconcerting, but always exciting and provoking'
THE OBSERVER

0 552 99204 6

BLACK SWAN

A SELECTED LIST OF FINE NOVELS
AVAILABLE FROM BLACK SWAN